məu'zeiik, or Q

K.I. JAGOBAN

ARCHWAY
PUBLISHING

Archway Publishing books may be ordered through booksellers or by contacting:

Archway Publishing
1663 Liberty Drive
Bloomington, IN 47403
www.archwaypublishing.com
844-669-3957

ISBN: 978-1-6657-0213-3 (sc)
ISBN: 978-1-6657-0214-0 (hc)
ISBN: 978-1-6657-0212-6 (e)

Library of Congress Control Number: 2021902092

Print information available on the last page.

Archway Publishing rev. date: 03/22/2021

Para mi fan numero uno, Indira 'Yoli' Olmos

Contents

God Emptied Us
Out to Earth

I t was Fayetteville the first time, a most horrible lie. And like all horrible lies, it made the cock crow. Now that cock was old and brown, so full of feathers and years it had a hop for a walk. Dutifully each morning, it would come to rouse the world around from slumber, and when rousing started, by God there was no stopping him. That morning wasn't any different. It flew on the fence like it had always done, looked around with the casual disdain of an overfed overlord, stretched out, flapped its wings, and crowed long and hard.

His heart flew. He pressed his palm to his phone speaker, but it was too late. It would have been futile even if it hadn't been. She had caught it and he knew she had because the pause that followed was of the dafuq? kind. It was their first call in a long time since they'd been texting, and now his tone began to falter and he began to feel a slow-winding, liquefying sensation in his guts that made him want to fold up and hang up. And all for what? A damn rooster. It would continue, he knew. He hung up and called back minutes later, only because it was suspicious not to. It was hardly seconds that he spoke before it let out long and hard again.

Again, a pause.

Before she asked him if that was what she thought she heard, she felt a degree of apprehension about his reaction, that he would think the question was implying something that stank. "A rooster?" he asked, countering her question. "A fuckin' rooster?" No, there was no fuckin' rooster, he said emphatically, a little mad that she would think he stayed where roosters did. Then he made up an excuse intended to shut her up, just like those he would continue to make along the way. She would think about this. He made it up the day a battalion of frogs gathered about the back of his house and brought hell down with their noise. He made up excuses for every strange honk and every chicken clucking, for every strange sound and every wildly crying child screaming in a language she knew could not possibly be English … He made up excuses till he told himself the truth about these noises in the background. He would lose her if he kept up with calling, so he stopped, and of course, she asked why. This time it was an excuse shrouded in the kind of lie so insulting and belittling to her intelligence that it would drive her to public records.

The public records couldn't lie, yet she kept herself from seeing the truth they presented for fear that her suspicions would be confirmed. She didn't want to lose him; that is why she didn't want to know. Yet she knew finding out on her own was a far better option than it revealing itself. Now, sitting there, as she became aware of her heartbeat, her fingers flying across the keyboard, working the letters of his name and his city one after the other till they made up the names of who he said he was and where he said he stayed, she waited those few short seconds, hoping, desperately so, that she was wrong.

The wait was a weight that sat on her lungs, confiscating her breath. It delivered its reply in caps, so bold in its assertion that whatever or whoever she was searching for did not, and had never, existed in that locality, ever. Something began to cave in her, like her innards were getting sucked into a sinkhole. She stared at the screen for a long time, the way you might look at a safe you don't expect to find empty. This had to be a lie. The public records had to be incorrect or the letters of his name had to be misspelled somehow. She erased the letters and retyped them, doubly careful now. Clicked. It turned up the same thing: that he didn't exist in that locality. He wasn't there. He had been lying about who he was. Now she felt like a mule had sent two kicks to her chest.

"Why her?" was the first question she asked. If he was untruthful with something as basic as who he was—his name—would what he said he did, what he said he felt, or what he said he would do hold any truth? There was no world they were both building. This wasn't the kind of truth she wanted to (or rather, expected to) know even if she wanted to know it. How could he not be who he said he was after all those months of saying he was coming back soon to paint a portrait of her last boy, to cradle her face in his hands each time they shared a kiss, to buy a house together, to build a life together? There was no way anyone could act so perfectly consistent. There was no way those lengthy texts meant nothing that they said. But then, the more she countered facts with these confusing resemblances to truth, the more facts, little as they were, insisted they further unearthed: how he placed the *u* in the word *color* every time they texted (she had shown it to her friend and she remembered the friend asking her if that guy was American); how his *t*'s and *d*'s came out crisp and never rolled when they spoke; how he asked the school year when any fool knew when it started and ended; how the business he claimed to own had no phone line, no website, no complimentary card; how he disappeared for days on end and resurfaced with a tale that the whole of his county had what he could best describe as a "brief county blackout."

3

She would wait for his call whenever he decided calling was safe and less deceitful, she decided.

He soon did when his texts went unanswered. She ignored the usual cheer in his tone and asked him where he was. The question came like the lunge from a cutthroat's knife, swift, with the kind of pointedness and unexpectedness that makes ducking, or dodging impossible.

"What do you mean where I am?" he shot back after a falter. "Are we still talking about this at this point in our relationship?"

"I'm just asking where you are," she said calmly.

The wrath in his tone had begun to build and thicken. He would teach her a lesson. So she had decided to imply something stinking, right? And say bye to their future because of baseless doubts, right?

"Baseless doubts?" she questioned. "Baseless doubts when—"

He hissed and hung up.

His mind was in a furious gallop where he was. Something was wrong. No one asked a person where he was if she didn't think he was there. She had fished something out, that woman. What exactly and the extent of it was what he was thinking when her text came. It was short—"I checked public records"—a bucket of ice over him. It would be many hours before his frozen anxiety would thaw, 'fore he'd reply. Those replies would come through spoken words, not texts. He would speak like a wounded man to a woman wounded. He was sorry, he said. He didn't mean to say half-truths and untruths, he said. He still loved her, he said, and cared about her.

When she asked him where he was, where he really was, he sighed.

"I just need the truth," she said through a whisper that urged. "I still love you too."

He loved her too. And he knew she meant it and that her hurt had not diminished as much as a speck of her love for him. Yet he knew that if he lied again, she would never ever believe him. He was a long way from her, farther than she would ever imagine he was. He never meant for it to end this way, but he would tell her all the same.

"Hello?" he heard her whisper and found himself coming back to the present.

She sighed.

He did too.

Then, "I am in Kent," he said. A pause. "England." That was the second time.

They say trust is like a paper sheet, something that can't be straightened out after it's been crumpled, that can never be the same. It was never quite the same after that. She had felt her heart fall into her stomach the moment she saw his status as a nonperson. She had driven home with her hands so tight around the steering wheel that the blood in them drained, leaving her knuckles bony and chalky, and she had walked into her home on legs numb as rubber, headed for her bed and her pillows. She would never cry in front of her boys, not even when the backs of her eyes burned. That night, her youngest came by her bedside to rub her feet.

"Are you all right, Mom?"

"*Si, papito,*" she'd quickly replied, smiling, smoothing back his hair. "*Vas a domir ahora?*"

"Yes." He seemed to be looking carefully at her, searching her face for the part that was a facade. "Why don't you call Sully?"

He was seven, looking so innocent. Things were simple in his world. The one plus one he knew gave you two. If Mommy was mad at him and his brothers, the solution was Sully, that guy who she texted, who made her smile. How then could she begin to explain that he wasn't real? Those were the kind of things that messed up a kid's mind. And it had taken all her strength to keep her composure without losing it, even long after the boy had hugged and kissed her and left.

She felt a fool for ever thinking she could get on a plane to meet the man she thought she knew who was just two hours' and a few states away. For thinking they'd fly to each other till they could live out the living arrangements they had talked about for so long. That would be one of the first times her love for him would be tested. Because when he said he wasn't in Georgia, she at least hoped it was another state or one close to it. She'd never expected another country. She'd never expected England or any place so far removed that only phone calls and momentary visits could do. England meant an entire new world a world away, a humongous shift in a lot of what she'd planned with him. But she still wanted to. There was a yearning in her that prompted her to text him the next morning and tell him good night the next night, and there was that part in her heart that convinced her that she could take that chance. If only he told the truth. And he had. It hadn't erased the hurt or demolished the walls that had reared or the questions she had chosen to suppress or ignore that had swum back afloat. It had simply put what was past behind. This, at least, was another starting point, but with creases.

"Namibia" happened in Fayetteville a mere month and the half into their "meeting." But before Namibia and the drama and disappointment that followed, before the $12,000 he demanded of her and her no that rigidly remained so, there was the gift card that came the fourth week in.

For a bosom friend stuck in the Ukraine, he had said, a model who needed all the help she could get in raising funds there, he needed $400. His colleagues were doing all they could to raise help. This was what he could do, so could she?

The moment he sent the request, he had noticed the. Sudden withdrawal and silence that set the tone for suspicion and hostility.

"Hello," he texted, contemplated sending, thought better of it, and wiped.

He saw her typing …

"Typing" disappeared and came back again, and he grew impatient, imagining if she had it to give it so he could help his model friend stuck in the Ukraine. Seconds turned to minutes.

"Do you have Walmart close to you?" she had asked.

Why was she asking that? Of course he had Walmart.

"Okay," she texted. "Go get it from there."

It was noon, and the sun was brutal the summer he asked for that gift card. Thirteen years ago he had come to this country and had become a photographer washing negatives. He was busy washing lots of negatives, he said. The sun was fucking hot, he said, again. And in Walmart, he said finally, pain in his voice, the cashiers always made a "mockery" of his "accent."

It was a bit too much, asking for $400 just because of three reasons, but it's like she did the math and sent him one. There was tension before she did. Something had stiffened her the moment he had asked for those gift cards. The story prompting the request was unlike anyone had ever told her. The normal storyline was a "sick relative". The reasons stuck too, even when she hadn't heard his accent at the time to believe him enough that it was something being made, or to be made, fun of. It confused her the more, because he made the request long after she had expected him to, when they had just "met," long after she forgot what he might be capable of.

Those before him had professed love immediately after "meeting," asking favors a few hours later, days maybe, a week for the stubbornest ones who held out the longest. But this, he didn't seem to need it because even after he had requested it, he hadn't replied to her silence to see what she thought of that kind of request, not even a hello. Yet he had asked, and whoever asked, for gift cards especially, was a Nigerian. A catfisher. A scam. It didn't matter that this one didn't fit the profile. He had asked and she had stiffened, and her heart had had a giant piece of her opinion of him chopped off because she was both uneasy and disappointed.

He still wasn't texting.

"I'll get it." That curtness cut finely like an ax. It carried in itself a message that no length of accusation or questioning could extract or rival. That was insult enough and he wasn't going to have it. So he burst into a torrent of angry words that cut her like a knife just the way hers had him. "If you think that because every idiot out there asking for gift cards is a scam," he began, "then it hurts, and is a disappointment that you fucking think that because I asked, to help someone I care about, you think I'm one of them. Not everyone who asks is a scam just because the ones who have turned out to be. You can keep it."

She stared at the words, conflicted, cut by how hard he had suddenly become and how callous those words were, for some reason. Who said anything about scams? She didn't want to "keep" it, yet she wanted to, not because she didn't want to give but because she didn't want to give someone she wasn't sure about. For all the guilt she felt, she remembered. That he had asked. People didn't just ask people they hadn't met for $400 or for anything. Yet he had a point.

Her eyes were twitching, and her face had gotten all red and blotchy, and her nose had begun to run. She was going to get $100 and nothing more for him, but this was going to be the last time, she swore. He swore that was going to be the last time. Then Namibia happened.

———

Now, Namibia. Two colleges had given him the go-ahead to source for artifacts. If he sourced for the right ones like he had previously successfully done with five other colleges, he would hit it big just before he made out time to come see her. He was broke, he said. He wanted to make sure he was "loaded" when he came to see his lady. Even if these colleges didn't purchase all of them, he told her, he could organize an exhibition and then an auction. He was leaving from Hartsfield-Jackson, he said, and staying for two weeks and not a day more. He left on a Thursday, arrived on a Saturday, called her the evening of that day, and started through Swakopmund on Monday, scouring. This was going to be his biggest job if he could pull it off, and whenever he said this, she knew he could do it because he was smart enough. He was fucking smart, she said, one of the things about him that turned her on. The colleges had to know he could pull this off before they awarded him this, yes? He would sigh from the day's work, and a yes would come hissing through text.

"I love you, *mi amor*," he would say.

"*Yo tambien te amo mucho*," she always replied.

He stayed in Swakopmund for two weeks like he said he would, sourcing, gathering, and sending pictures of rare finds.

"I am proud of you," she said. "I told you you could."

But at the end of two weeks, he made a grand mess of everything, including himself, by getting himself into the kind of trouble that only $12,000 could solve. She had a vague idea of the "mess" because he never said much about it and she had a feeling it was far from indeliberate. Only that the artifacts had been purchased, that his work there had been done, and that the only problem was $12,000 to bring them home. The moment she heard "twelve thousand," her guts began to clench. She could be wrong, but she knew where this was going. There was that sensation that ruled her consciousness each time her heart began to chip away at the edges, and where her heart chose to stay silent, her head kept on saying, "I told you so! I told you so!!"

"So what do you need?"—Thu. 7:31 p.m.

He paused: typing … typing … "Twelve will be enough."—Thu. 7:37 p.m.

"I don't have it"—11:16 a.m. Sat.

It was the kind of no so deaf and unyielding it might as well have been dead. Do you talk to dead things?

He did.

"I don't have any other option. You are the only option, my only one."

It was what he kept saying. A week had passed already. The colleges had begun to call, he told her. If he messed up in this, his track record and reputation would be destroyed. But he could have been talking to a piece of thing for all the world cared. She found not entirely believable that the success of a project of this scale would come to rest on her assistance. Like she had been part of the plan when he was making applications to them.

She told him once, "I can't be your only option. If we hadn't started chatting, what would you have done?" He fell silent. When he spoke at last, he flew into such a rage she feared for her own life. It was then that she knew he was telling lies that sounded so true only because she had believed so much of what he had said for her suddenly not to. It was that she was sure her hearing was good and she could still hear that fucking rooster crowing somewhere in "Namibia"'s background. It was that she found it ridiculous for a first-timer to travel on a one-way ticket.

The second week passed.

On the third week he called. It was early and unexpected, like him. His voice was low and beaten, and her concern spiked. He spoke slow and long. He didn't mean for this to happen or for him to ask her or for things to go south. He was sorry, he said. He would manage however he could and get through this.

They both said nothing for a long time. He asked for nothing. "I can't do $12,000," she said at last. "I can only do $500. How do I send it?"

He thanked her so much that she could feel his relief.

"How do I send it?" she asked again.

The question stayed unanswered till the next morning. He gave her a name and an address. Neither was his. The name was female. The address was to another, in the UK. She kept staring at them, hurt replaying in her heart. It was either of two things: either he wsn't in Namibia or he had a wife or some woman. The knots in her guts had started squeezing. She walked to the door on unsteady feet and shut it tightly behind her, leaning against the knob for momentary support. She felt light-headed. She crept into bed and huddled into a ball with her face in her arms between her knees because none of her boys should see her cry.

He called. He would keep up the calls. This would be the first in a string of calls. "It hurts that you do this every time …," he began after she had brought a hail of questions crashing on him, "… that you doubt me whenever it is financial. I've always said assumption is the lowest form of knowledge, but you never ever did listen. Now let me explain.

"People know I'm stuck here. My colleagues know I am. I've not been sitting on my ass doing nothing. Everyone is doing their quota to assist me. Everyone can't just send me money. They send it to"—and this is where the lady came in—"Stephanie" and she sends it down to me. You assume without asking questions. This is what you'll get. The very wrong thoughts."

That afternoon, cash in hand and info in head, a thought occurred to her. She checked first, the cost of sending money directly to Namibia; then she checked the cost to the UK. The UK was significantly higher. Yet he insisted she send it to the UK, to one Stephanie? It made no sense. Those were the kind of lies that maddened her, and it appeared like he was hardly off of one before he began concocting another.

The money was rolled in her hand. She noticed her hand grow unsteady as she filled out the slip and handed the money and the slip to the cashier. In minutes, she was done and she turned home. In her heart, there was now a conviction. It was like he had gotten what he wanted and she now had the authority to demand what she wanted, only that this wasn't backed by curiosity but by a need for the kernel of this truth, which had proven elusive hitherto, to be caught and broken. He would come back from Namibia, or say he had. She would say nothing and do nothing but wait. Until that day when he would call, when he would say his truth, when Kent would happen.

PART II

"B-u-e-n-o-s d-i-a-s, my sweet man!"

It was a text from her the morning after Kent.

These were the kind of texts that followed the mornings of the weeks after Kent when the tension had finally eased and they had slipped back into the warmth of mutual familiarity.

A smile broke his face into a moon, yet there was unease the size of a fist in his heart because she had asked him his house address in Kent some five nights ago and he simply had a feeling the request wasn't casual, even though it came thrown that way. He knew she believed him now. There was no greater relief than that. But somewhere in his heart he knew she hadn't entirely let her guard down. There were still seeds of mistrust that his actions had to eliminate, and these actions had to be consistent and progressive.

The realization that he had begun doing these things from the same place in his heart he treated himself with amused him at first. He knew he had a fondness for her, *si*. They had only met online. Never in person. Never even through a video call because she simply believed him enough not to request for one, even after Kent had come. This, hers, was a kind of trust that took him off guard because he was from a place where mistrust was the stamp your birth first gave you, then your culture, where hell had become so normal it was room temperature. Amusement had led to surprise.

"Do you know one of the toppest reasons I love you?" she had asked him once. "Because you listen." Surprised, because he was actually realizing he was interested in her and her affairs, it had been a long time coming. Surprise had led to slight anger. And slight anger had led to passive curiosity on where this mysterious, winding journey would lead. Yes, he had lied, but only when he had to, never because he simply wanted to, at least, until Namibia and the *dinero*. Those lies were calculated to predate when he first met her. Time had passed and, like all lies have to constantly be stacked to sound true, they had built. Now he was choiceless because as much as he wanted to say some things and clear some falsities, he knew that doing so was a risk that could tear them apart, and by God, he didn't want that, even if that meant stacking lies further to live in fantasy longer. Somewhere in his mind, he knew that bubble would pop. That moment hadn't come, and he hoped it wouldn't. So he simply gave her the address.

———

Something had begun "not to smell nice" in this whole affair again. Why was his address coming now? She swooped up through pages of their chats. She stopped at that point, copied the date, did a swift calculation, and landed at five. No normal, sincere human had to think five days where his address was. And *si*, she knew he was sure thinking about it because who would remember a casual question from a chat five days ago? A lot of people, maybe, but in this case, highly unlikely. Something had begun chumping through her belly. They were those knots that fisted so sudden and so tight. Those chain-sawing cramps that came, that sharpened and clung when someone genuinely loved cheated after apologizing, again. He couldn't possibly have lied again. No. Again she found herself not wanting to know if that was a lie, and again she worked up the courage to bullshit that feeling.

There was only one option left to know if that was the truth or if she was being played. It was an option that shrug-sneered, that seemed to say, "You said, again? That you had trust?" It was

Google. She would check where he said he stayed. As she typed the words, she found herself going back to that time in the past when she had done this, and those memories came back, hovering, haunting. The page sped toward result in an instant. It looked like a cottage flanked by two fairly tall buildings. Perhaps that would explain the rooster (that she still sometimes heard) after Kent began but chose to ignore. The results eased the cramps but would not clear them. That could be an inhabited cottage (or whatever it was) all right, but did that mean he was there? He had called her insecure. That slashed! Her sons had considered her fears irrational. That hurt! Sometimes she considered herself simply looking for his lies for no reason. Yet she couldn't shake that feeling that cottages in central Kent couldn't possibly have roosters standing to make a nuisance of their silly selves to the A&R firm beside it. She absolutely knew he was in London, of that she had no doubt. His accent was already enough evidence of that. Where exactly he was, she would not know, and she would have no idea why she thought that or why he was doing that until few days later. He came with a story.

When his mother died and paralysis dealt his father easily to the grave like valueless playing cards, his story went, it was this aunt, who was now in jail for unpaid debts, who stood for him and reared him before social security could bind him and put him on a truck bound for the largest London poorhouse, where skinheads are many and as vicious as they come. He was forever grateful, he said. Now this aunt was in debt with the creditor who breathed down her neck just hours ago but came back to satisfy the urge to ignore her pleas and make a misery out of her. He just needed her bailed. She was eighty-one, he said, sounding desperate. They could worry about raising money later.

Again, he was asking. This asking, there was something about it that managed to rattle her trust in him to the core, which had begun to fidget even when she hadn't realized it. But he needed it, and see, she had it. She didn't have everything he was asking for, the whole £900, but she could give what she had for his aunt and his electricity and water bills he had grouched about some days back.

"Give me your details. I'll send it after work. The details, please?"

He began to type.

And in her heart, she began to pray.

It was a prayer that had chased hope and hoped it wasn't in vain. It was the strange kind of prayer that prayed for wrong, her being wrong.

He would type and then stop. Her heart would halt. Then he would type, keep typing, and stop.

The details were a certain Stephanie whose surname she could still recall quite clearly, the city too. It had become very clear.

―――――――――

One day passed, one day after she went ahead, despite what she felt, to send the money. That day was shaded amber. Rain fell in it, soaking it, freeing an army of termites. It was a beautiful day to lose someone. Both said absolutely nothing.

She had stared at the details so long and hard, they had become imprinted in her mind. She had cried till she spent what last pence could get strength get it. She had been played again. She had seen these things coming, but she had been fooled with her eyes open. The torture of that had built and hacked. She had said nothing to him afterward. Not a word. The chats lay empty for one more day.

But before he had typed the details, he had paused. There was a battle in him. Without thinking, he typed and sent, hoping the fantasy could go a little further. If he had thought, he wouldn't have. He waited for her reply. Five minutes. Ten. Thirty. His heart began to tell him. Three hours. A day.

The next day, without a word but good luck, she sent the receipt of payment to him. That shocked him. What was happening? She was saying nothing like she had finally caught wind, yet she was doing it exactly like she had not a clue. Paranoia stalled his hands from opening the message to reply. Two days. He instinctively, without any doubt, knew that she knew now. Slight anger had turned to passive curiosity. Now she was gone, and fear and dread had descended on him because she was. On the morning of the third day, he sent a message. There was something he wanted to tell her, he said. There was no reply.

This was the second time, and it hurt and stung at the same time. Hurt and sting were all she felt when she heard the name that had come to replay itself in her head. Costello.

PART III

The man who called himself Costello began like this: "I am ready to tell you the truth now … but know this: you changed my life and you made me smile."

Her 'icon' fell below his message. That meant she had read it. He began his truth.

17

He had started this as a game. It had become serious. He had become hooked to her, and the truth was that he loved her. "I know you know all this already," he texted.

"The only thing I know is that you're in London," she said, a crack in her voice. "Nothing more."

"No, I'm not," he said.

"Where are you?" she said.

He began to type.

"I am in Nigeria."

PART IV

"At least let me see who I've been talking to."

If his mind had a nose, it sure would've twitched. This rat carried too much smell for it to go unnoticed. He had toiled in this shithole. Now here was someone who loved him and did so thoroughly, someone who wanted nothing but the truth from him, which, if not for his stubbornness, he would have given. He thought of his mother. If things worked out between him and her, he could go over to Dallas with her and help his mother be better through far better work conditions. He could be somebody, something, with her.

"Oloye, at least let me see who I'm talking to," she said again, because he had told her his name and his surname.

It was a request that was not to be delayed. He had delayed once. It had turned out to be a lie.

"Promise me," he said, "would you promise you will not report me to the authorities?"

"I promise you I will not," she said.

He thought of his mother. It would kill her if he were ever taken. He looked at her words. Tried to detect any deceit or hurt poised to strike back in them. Saw nothing.

He navigated his gallery, went to photos, selected one of his, and then just tapped and sent without thinking. He watched it load in a circle, wondering if he had just killed his mother. It loaded in another quick second and then appeared in her inbox. Then he began to wait.

Her message icon fell below his message. That meant she had seen it.

"That's you, right?" she texted. She was looking at him, brown face, brown hair, a scowl, no older than twenty-two. So this was the one who had macheted her world right through the middle. She was looking at him and remembering the kind of things that makes people's eyes twitch.

There was something unusual about that question. Just something. His wariness increased.

"Yes."

Nothing.

He typed again, "???"

Her icon kept falling below his messages. Then she said, "Okay."

19

Paper Hostages:
The Jericho of Hope

There were ninety students in there that morning, but all ninety counted for shit because 'in there' was silent as shit. We had come upon these rumors that punched, crumpled, and twisted the guts. Today was the day we were going to confirm, to sieve the authenticities from the mendacities, and to hope to God that the former was palatable. At the front were the teachers who, too, stood solemn. Ms. Rachel, English language teacher, tall and bespectacled with that pair of heavy, confident, lifted-at-the-tip boobs we all loved. Ms. Omoduwa, biology teacher, short, haphazardly created and relatively insignificant, a perfect gargoyle. Mr. Oraka, maths teacher, with the suddenly compressed head, body as compact and thick as yesterday's fufu. Mr. Uwaifo, further maths teacher, horribly dressed as usual, shapeless as a flung rug … and the rest of the staff.

Then the arrogant malafacka walked in, principal and proprietor Ikoku, with his signature head made of the shape, size, and shine of moon, his presence deepening the hush, heightening the pressure. The SS II line, all the humans in it, stiffened to straight-backed attention, the ones not a hundred percent sure of themselves careful to conceal themselves. For this man was a faultfinder, a martinet, and most frightening, a being with a tempestuous temper.

Ikoku stood. Surveyed from over the top of his spectacles for any one he might harangue. Satisfied then (or dissatisfied), he murmured his greeting, "Good morning, students."

The assembly's greeting emerged from the silence as a great, stretching beast. "Goood moooorning, sir!" And collapsed back into it.

"How was your night?"

It was a sweeping mumble for a reply. "Fiiiine, siiir!

"Hmm!" He cleared his throat and cracked a rambling joke about a certain horse that only understood the words, "in Jesus's name" and "amen." There was a hanging, resounding silence at the end of it, almost embarrassing. We laughed on sudden cue, giving him more heartiness than his joke deserved before shutting back our voices as fast and sudden as we had laughed, aching to hear the news.

"You have probably heard the news," he began almost with a sigh, "about you SS II students, especially." He pulled off his specs and fingered his lips with one of the handle tips, looking straight at us unfortunates. "You will be writing WAEC soon, less than a year from now. Mathematics and English, as the wise ones know, are of the utmost importance." He shrugged and smirked. "We cannot let you people move on to the next level if you have not mastered at least the two basic pillars of that level. You will only succeed in failing terribly, failing like you were ordained to, failing WAEC and NECO, failing and flinging slime and disrepute to this highly distinguished school that senators and reps, governors, ambassadors … counselors bring and want to bring their children to." He smiled a thin, self-satisfied smile.

See, there was the time to rain curses on him for that nonsensical last statement, but this was not the time. We would do that later. Something else was more important now. We were literally holding our breaths, waiting for the bombshell.

He pointed to the SSS III line. "You know the mistake? The mistake we made with most of these animals is that we let them slip from grasp, from their zoos of unintellect, when they knew absolutely nothing in either maths or English." There was a shuffling of sandals from that line for having been called animals, but no more than that. He continued. "We made the grave error of nursing optimism that they would put in extra work when they got to where they now are. But no, my teachers are the ones suffering now, complaining bitterly because even the most rudimentary formulas, one plus one, most of them would have to count on their fingers. It is only to pursue girls and go to parties they know, drinking like thirsty laborers, smoking cancer-enhancing hemp. But one plus one, most of the animals don't know. Now my staff have to go back, wasting valuable time, trying to hammer knowledge and sense into reinforced blocks. Are we making that mistake anymore? We are not making that mistake anymore."

"If," he continued, "you SS IIs think you can be promoted to SS III without passing maths and English, you are utterly fooling yourselves."

The bombshell had detonated. Had ripped apart the earth from under us and pulled us in it. Ikoku could be anything, but one thing we all knew was that he didn't appear in front of his students to sound empty warnings. He was an arrogant man. He cared more about his school's prestige than the number of students. He wielded the capacity to stagnate anyone in a class if he deemed it fit to. If the parents thought otherwise, he calmly explained the value of mastery, and if they resorted to begging or making promises that the student be given a chance, he became brash, declining, showing them the door, quite literally and figuratively. Though rare, he had done it to a few dumb-as-a-rock students. But now, here he was, making the rare a rule. There were just a handful of students in SS II who knew both subjects well enough to pass and be promoted. Maths was the major beast that gored the most of us down. Whoever didn't know English well enough to pass it was a dunce. So we had to pass maths too? No, that couldn't work.. This man had to be joking. Or at least, that is what we told ourselves to bolster hope.

"If you pass the rest of the subjects and fail either maths or English, you are going nowhere. No teacher is going back to start teaching any unserious animal something he should have mastered this year or the year before. No unserious animal is dragging us back. No unserious animal is tarnishing our prestige. Do you hear me?"

Our silence was more out of shock than resentment. His authority, his charge, had to be affirmed.

"Do you hear me, SS II students?" he barked.

"Yes, sir."

"Good!" He smiled his thin smile, turned, and walked away.

Silence spread and tucked us in like sheets.

Black Cornelius was from the sunniest town in the Congo and nobody knew exactly who had started that rumor. His real name was Sikoukou. Black and shiny as freshly sloughed mamba, so thin he could run through half-shut doors, with a face capable of frightening stiffs out of caskets, he was one strange specimen of a boy. He had largely been derided and altogether ignored hitherto, but girls had suddenly started sitting on his lap, letting a few buttons down, nibbling at his ears, jostling for the empty seats beside him and shocking the poor black man to embarrassment.

This egghead that had his nerd head perpetually in a book, his push pen incessantly *click-clicking* in his hands and twirling around his fingers had guillotine-sharp brains that lasered through impossibly huge, abstract pyramids of calculations and equations, poking, cracking and crumbling them bit by bit till they Jerichollapsed as rubble at his feet. He spoke a distant and perverted form of English, but his essays and letter writing in English language class wound up with professorial polish. No one knew how he did it. No one cared. You didn't get cookies for being all that smart in our school (because nearly everyone was reasonably smart). You got them for being smart, social, and fashionable, especially (and emphatically) in reverse order.

But Black Cornelius's time had come for of the handful of people who knew both subjects to the core, the one or two generous enough to pass knowledge and the handful who could actually pass knowledge, Black Cornelius was the most—if not the only—self-effacing, seemingly malleable one, the one who almost everyone turned to for their ticket to the next level. Girls began to show him copious love. Like I said, they licked his ears. An ear lick was a dangerous thing, a ploy cooked in hell's kitchen, in its stuffiest cauldron, something that restructured (destructured, really) men's thoughts, making them (Sikoukou, in this case) talk almost as ceaselessly as a canary would sing. And guys showed him brotherly love.

At first he taught for free, crowded from all sides, especially by the best of the girls, who left their boyfriends during both long and short break for—"Where the sloppy fuck are you going to?"—Sikoukou's corner. His personal simplicity and reservoir of flexible solutions for rigid problems contributed more to their understanding a little more than anything else he did, embellishing his legend. This went on for two straight weeks. Well, before the pride of long deferred recognition perched on his soul and built a nest there so that on the third week, he demanded payment (which boys did give), on the fifth week for trysts (which girls shut their eyes and gave), and on the sixth week for worship (which people contemplated), resulting in the seventh week when Almighty God, in a fit of … of … jealousy or whatever fit God is known to throw, took drastic action and punished him properly with a venereal. Poor Sikoukou! He came back some three weeks later, slow, stooped, saturnine, and suspicious, convinced that a coven of witches in that class had done him in, curtly rebuffing every appeal to spread his knowledge, even with promises of more sex, more payment, and worship.

So once again, the hope of the many, especially people like Arhe "Buns Pie" Okomu, Moses "Dirty Gum" Akpotietiemunor, Doro "High Chief" Agata, and myself, were smashed.

<hr />

"See am, e beta you continue dey cast, cast die, make you know say dem don ordain your seat for hellfire, dan for you to try form holy, come still jam hellfire o."

Exactly what I heard Doro saying when I ran into him and Oshodi seriously playing tennis upstairs when maths class was going on downstairs. It was a fortnight until exams, and there was a lot of sense in that. Better I ignored the threat of failure and played, harder even, than trying to get serious about it just weeks to the exam, depriving myself of fun and still failing. I shrugged.

"After sack, na me," I said and sat beside Friday and Arhe, whose faces were cupped gloomily in their palms. "Ha fa nah?"

No reply.

I forgave, for I understood.

The ball did its poh-ki-teh from bat to board and board back to bat with languorous speed. And when Oshodi finally decided to cut the travesty, to smash the ball so hard it flew and landed a hundred thousand miles away, rolling smoothly across the floor instead of bouncing, Doro glared at him like he had been betrayed and just wanted to shoot him right there and watch him bleed.

They joined us, silent for a bit, preferring this sloth to the horror downstairs that neither of us wanted to talk about or know about.

"Bring your phone na. Make we hear some soul-uplifting music."

Oshodi brought out his China phone called Bluetooth, and together we ended up watching *Massive Attack*. It was blonde porn. Not a pleasant sight, so we opted for *Ms. Ebony Gets a Creampie*, where we saw an authoritative black cock and a docile pink pussy we could all easily relate with. Both pornstars were lying sideways, one of the actress's thighs in the air, jism skimming thinly along the baton-size pummeling her.

Arhe stood up after a moment like he was disinterested, but his bulge, like a stretched bow, betrayed him. In that state there was only one thing he was going to do. Furiously denying secret perverseness (when we hadn't even accused him, by words at least) he walked round and round before stylishly strolling out.

"See am," we whispered. "E wan go throw dice now."

"Wanker."

Only for him to flee back less than a half a minute later, carefully but swiftly shutting the door behind him.

His bulge was gone. His eyes were wild, instinctively ordering silence and drawing like terror from us. What was it? Who was it? Was it Ikoku strolling up? If it was, how close was he, so we would start hurling ourselves from the windows down the three-story school? He swung, peeping through the door. Silently, we joined him. Old Man Imoni, the school's official, most important secretary, who appeared only before and during exams, was walking down. He stopped, seeming to sense the presence of people. For a couple of seconds he stood still, appearing to sniff, making our hearts pound loudly. But then he turned, cocked his head, walked some more, unwound the lock of the burglary proof gate, turned the knob of the main door of his office, and pushed. In his hand was a sheaf of papers. He paused again before walking in.

Horror had placed us all in a cast. We could not afford to be seen, just as we could not afford to stay a moment longer. He could decide to walk down to the hall. See us. Report us to Ikoku. The consequences for skipping class, maths class for that matter, when all of us obviously were the animals that knew jack shit in maths especially after his assembly talk just a few weeks ago, would be off the charts. Finally, we decided to brave it. We would make the fifteen-yard walk from the hall to his office as quietly as possible, bend the corner, and make a dash. One by one, on tiptoes, we moved, and as soon as we were past his office, we fled right down the flight of stairs two and three at a time to join the maths class.

Now, Doro, in addition to being a rebel and a natural ferreter of easy things, was a shrewd opportunist, and like all shrewd opportunists, he was a chronic observer. But I will talk about that later.

Sitting in class side by side, the both of us (and I'm sure a lot others) bored deaf and driven distant by the endless talk and mountain of digits piling up on the board, we longed to leave again. To the toilet. To the library. To anywhere but this torture chamber.

"I rather cut grass dan stay class," I whispered to Doro, but he didn't laugh. Strange, because he normally laughed at statements that supported hooky. I nudged him to laugh. He didn't. I glanced at him. He seemed lost in thought, and he was never lost in thought except when he was thinking about mischief and the execution of it.

The climate in the class was one of fear, of despair, and of the desperate hope doomed men cling to: people frantically penning formulae, copying from each other, literally leaning forward, ears standing like antennae, brows furrowing, the madness of confusion reigning supreme. Black Cornelius seemed to relish it. He had turned out to be more of a bastard than we had thought. He was more vocal nowadays, actually going to the front of the class and proffering solutions to complex problems. In that haughty hunch of his shoulders when he walked back, that arched brow when praise was given, he seemed to say, "Na my time be dis! Haters, park well."

"Dah boy go chop slap without cutlery after school today," I whispered Doro who said "eh" very absentmindedly.

Mr. Oraka was still chalking yet another equation on the board. The mood in the class had collapsed completely now. Few people were writing. When the bell rang, the mass exodus was enough evidence that nobody wanted to have sense again, that they had damned the new rules and resigned themselves to fate.

Doro nudged me and signaled with his head. That meant the toilet. What could this mischief be now? We had stolen a carton of Capri Sonnes the other day and drunk it in a hurry, and when we emptied them in the art studio, unaware that the art teacher was there, he had yelled, "Hey, come here!" to catch the culprits, and we had fled. We had searched people's bags when they were out and palmed whatever cash they unwisely left there, sometimes rolling into the thousands. We had opened people's food flasks and ate their meat and/or fish and, in sudden thought of cruelty, left the chewed bones right in there. We had raided the school library and stolen encyclopedias, Guinness records and novels that promised fun to stock our private libraries with. We had raided the art gallery too, stolen paintings, carvings, and drawings and trekked to Hausa Quarters to exchange them for footwear and Bluetooth headphones. We—and some guy called Martins—had decided to lock up a particularly new, obnoxious teacher in her office at the close of school so that she nearly spent the night in there. We had threatened and obtained a couple of white girls, who we decided had to pay National Fees and International Student Resident School Fees because they were staying in our country and schooling in our school. We had captured a boy and beaten him soundly because we had forewarned him to change the style and reduce the volume of his laughter. We had planned all these in the toilet. So what now? I followed him down.

"Dis tin wey I wan tell you so," he began. "No tell am anybody."

I nodded.

Then he told me he was planning to steal some exam question papers. "English and maths, dah maths especially wey wan give us wahala…" to "take them hostage…"

Paper Hostages:
The Spirit of Ikoku

These were the kind of decisions criminals wished they had never made.

I wriggled my finger in my ear several times and tilted the ear to him. "Talk wetin you talk again?" Because, by God, I knew he was joking. Knew he had to be joking. Knew I couldn't believe I'd heard that correctly; that, in the brief seconds we had seen Old Man Imoni standing there, trying to sniff us out, while we were thinking of running and saving our skins, his criminal mind had instead been thinking of how to get right into the office and take question papers hostage.

"E no hard, see? Imoni no dey lock door. You no see am? E open door before e enta? You no see?" The forked tongue of a snake. The smooth unfurling of uncertainty made certain and backed with reason. He was talking faster, his words halting my protests, circumventing them, his lips moving faster. He talked, his neck appearing to skip from side to side. If the world were a farmful of animals (as it is), he would have been the pig, Squealer.

"We fit run am? You no dey see?" And each and every time he said, "You no see?" or "You no dey see?" I actually saw, and like he sensed that his ability to inspire seeing had been connected to, he seized tightly upon it, revving the intensity till it steamed, stoking the flames till it burst, garnishing the vision with step-by-step actions, right from the execution on to its completion and success.

"I go be d lookout, I go stand for stepcase dey observe if anybody dey come. Na you go fall-in d office, locate am, snap every-every, move ahead. E no hard. You no dey see? We go dissolve all d equation, all the calculation sharperly, we go fall-in hall, scatter every-every, when result come out, we go win, fall-in SS III. Abi, you wan repeat?"

I said no, that God forbid I repeat.

"No be matter of God forbid," he spat severely. "Na you yourself go fit forbid bad tin, shey you see?"

He had convinced me completely, the confidence man. But one thing I hadn't fallen for: the part where I had to be the one to go into the office to "snap every-every."

"You know wetin?" I said.

"Wetin?"

"No be me go enta office."

He sighed and his voice took on that low, honeyed modulation of serpents that would quickly turn swift. With a hand on my shoulder, he began: "See, e no hard …"

The longer I stayed there listening to his tongue wag in my ear, the more convinced I would be to partake in an action that I had not thought up but to which the heaviest of punishments would be appropriated. "No!" I near-yelled.

He stared helplessly at me. The finality with which I had said it had come with a force heavy enough to convince him that it was going to be a waste of breath trying to convince me.

"Okay." He sighed.

"Okay, what?"

"We go use Buns Pie."

mə

If I was expecting him to say he would do it himself, I was disappointed. Bastard, he was. He was my friend, but he was a devious bastard.

———

Arhe "Buns Pie" Okomu was one of the worst hit. Okomu knew little as was evident in his favorite verbal abuse, the one that ended up becoming his nick. He had barely escaped SS I. Now, with the announcement, he knew his days of formal education were coming to an uneventful end. The look on his face after the announcement was unforgettable. "Horrid," as people who saw him would later say (and draw hope from), "like a kid tossed off a carousel into a pit."

Everyone knew Arhe was going to drop out after his WAEC. Even Arhe did deep down and he accepted it. What he couldn't accept was not being able to go on to SS III to peacefully write his WAEC and dropout. He was dropping out either way but somehow, being a preschool cert dropout instead of a school cert dropout had to sting harsher. Doro knew this.

"We go use Buns Pie. Na d perfect man for d job," Doro said again.

We didn't need to look for him. We went straight to the place where we'd find him: the canteen. He was eating with both hands, his mouth stuffed and his temple veins furiously doing gbim-gbim-gbim. Perhaps this was the problem, I reasoned. He ate too much. His brain had been clogged and insulated with food. He thought in terms of food. He slept while others reasoned, and now, if we didn't help him help himself, he was going to be yet another one of the rare wastes both life and death would reject. The disgust on my face was the lesser of the one on Doro's. Perhaps he had sensed that two pairs of eyes were upon him, for he stopped, eyes suspicious, brows furrowed, cheeks puffed on both sides with food. He turned and growled with the utmost anger. "Wetin una two dey ozzav me for nah?"

We smiled. "Ah braa, nuttin nah. Shuoo!'"

He didn't like the answer he got, didn't like the fact that we had suddenly turned up, because these two together, he had probably thought, were usually up to no good. And he didn't want to be on the receiving end of any mischief they might concoct. So he simply hurriedly swallowed the food in his mouth and packed up what was left on the table. That was the end of him in the canteen. But we looked at ourselves, shrugged, and subsequently began to tail him. He was the ticket for himself to the next level as much as he was for us. If he decided to be a fool at this crucial moment, we would force him to be wise, either with words or a whip. If he decided to be foolish afterward, that was solely up to him.

He looked back again. And again. And again-again. The moment he saw us, perhaps seized by his fear of the unknown, he began to run. Where he was running to when we were going to end up seeing each other in class, we didn't know. This was yet one fantastically foolish aspect of the animal we were to deal with, we concluded and gave up hope on him. He was no good, our gestures said, and we made him see those gestures by not looking in his direction for most of the remaining hours we spent in class. At the close of school, when he least expected it, as he whistled away, two iron hands—ours—seized both of his arms. Before he could start yelling (for this is the path brainless cowards resort to when consumed by sudden uncertainty), we shoved him into the toilet, a hand clamped over his mouth, and lectured him sternly for ten minutes before taking him into our confidence and painstakingly worming ourselves into his. Slowly, he calmed down and we began, Doro building up the structure and me slapping beef on the few parts that creaked.

"Serious matta? Make we go move am now nah?"

We knew we had won when we saw his eyes shine, when his mouth fell open, when his ears seemed to twitch with his word, when he finally found his voice and said, "Serious matta? Make we go move am now nah?" Such was his eagerness. This was good! Very good! But we had to literally restrain him from running upstairs, packing whatever papers he saw (relevant to us or not), and running home with them.

Soon after he had parted from us, as we walked home, Doro said to me, "I hope say e no go spoil our parole, put us for trouble o. Because dah boy sense neva cake well."

I agreed with him.

It was one thing to be eager; it was another to be desperate. Apart from the spellings, they differed. Especially when placed within the grasp of a dangerous fool, the likes of which we now had in our hands to manage.

The building was three stories, so there were six flights of stairs. On the ground floor was JSS I–III, the junior staff room, the canteen, and the malafacka, Ikoku's office. On the second story was SS I–III, yet another staff room, the toilet (our meeting place), the art studio, and the library. On the third story was the assembly hall, the science lab, and Old Man Imoni's office. The teachers had confirmed, through inference or otherwise, that their exam question papers had been submitted. Old Man Imoni was frequenting school now, meaning he was typing the question papers. Further observance, strengthening our conviction to steal those papers, was the fact that Imoni, as frequently as he was coming to school was almost as frequently leaving the office to attend to the teachers, his stomach, or any number of things.

Examination timetables had been released. This was the week before exams, the revision week. The fever in SS II had toppled, the fear tripled. But for us three, this was the exact time to execute.

The plan was simple. We would wait till lesson time. Lesson time came after the formal close of school, when there were fewer students who needed extra tutorials. This would drastically reduce the risk of being seen. Doro would stand on the staircase of the second floor as a lookout for those coming up from the first floor and anyone possibly approaching from the second floor, occasionally making the rounds. I would stand on the staircase leading to the third floor in such a way that I'd be within reasonable distance of Doro and Arhe so the former could see and communicate quickly and clearly to me if anyone was coming too close and the latter would be informed in the same fashion to pull out. All hope was staked on Arhe now—his speed, his agility, his discernment, and most importantly, his carefulness.

The day was Monday. We had three days remaining should Monday fail, because there were no lessons on Friday. And Monday ultimately did fail because for some reason Old Man Imoni stayed in the office right from assembly time to the close of lessons. Tuesday, the same thing happened. The reasons unraveled: With six classes worth of exam questions and him being the sole secretary, he was trying furiously to be on schedule. On Wednesday, the same thing happened. We had staked all our hopes on this. We had even stopped reading altogether. Now this? Panic started to set in. It got to the point that Doro turned to me to ask if we shouldn't just "playfully strangle Old Man Imoni." I looked at him and said nothing. If Doro thought it, he meant it.

In the toilet on Wednesday afternoon, as we contemplated, Arhe jumped from place to place, making whimpering sounds, looking like he wanted to die right where he stood. If we had let him, he would have run right into Old Man Imoni's office, hit him over the head multiple times, and snapped up every paper he could possibly lay hands on. Because that look on his face, that was desperation at its peak. So what were we going to do now?

For the good part of an hour, with Doro occasionally going to check out the office, me thinking, and Arhe whimpering, a thought suddenly occurred to me. Old Man Imoni typed the papers and operated the power supply. What if we shut down the power supply? It was located on the first floor anyway. Frustrated, he would leave his office and go down, and we would immediately take position and take the papers hostage. It wasn't much of a plan, but at least it was one. It would be extremely risky. We would have little time to search for and snap up as many as five to six exam papers, and we would have to be out of the way before he climbed back up. Arhe couldn't do it, I decided. I would do it. For the first time, I saw the tenseness on Doro's face relax. Doro would still be the lookout. Arhe would have to go down to shut the power supply off and find a way to not be seen. He mumbled, mopped sweat off his forehead and chin and agreed.

So on that day, in that toilet of criminal-minded fourteen-year-olds, we decided that we were going to be promoted to SS III whether the devils or Ikokus liked it or not, by hook or by crook. The whole school was quiet, the voices of diverse teachers in diverse classes floating to us from the distance. The bulb above us was shining.

"Arhe, na your hand e dey o," Doro said, slapping a hand on his shoulder. "Activate, no time. You know where power supply box dey abi?"

Arhe shut his eyes and took a deep breath. "Yes." He was out the door before we knew it. Arhe might have been academically dull, but he sometimes exhibited acts of 'bravery'. That was a redeeming factor we deeply respected.

A minute passed. Two minutes. My heart was pounding. Two and the half minutes. The low, whirring sound that accompanied the electricity began to sink even lower. The bulb above us flickered and slowly shrunk dim till it put itself out. We looked at ourselves. It was time.

———

Faintly, we heard the UPS beep. There was an angry groan. Imoni's. A handful of seconds passed. The gate whined and stayed silent. At that moment, Arhe rushed over. Fear had made his face ugly. Had he been caught? Had someone seen him?

"Wetin be dat?" Doro and I asked.

"Ikoku car dey outside," he whispered.

The shock both froze and shook us.

"Ikoku car?" I asked, shaking him.

"You sure say na Ikoku car?" Doro asked.

"I swear."

"But Ikoku no dey come school at dis time nah," Doro said adamantly, so adamantly that it almost seemed he wished that adamance to change Arhe's statement.

But Arhe was similarly adamant and sure. He stiffly brought his head up and down like the town lizard, shining his eyes. "Ikoku car dey dere. I no like dis business again."

I decided I didn't like this business too. Because, see, Ikoku moved like a damned spirit. He owned the school and he knew it well, down to the extent of knowing which parts of the floor to step on to cushion his movements. Plus, he seemed to sniff out mischief. Too many times, as students misbehaved while their teachers' backs were turned, there would suddenly be silence. For the ones carried away, refusing to recognize the sudden silence, it wasn't until a seat mate nudged them to be quiet, to behave, that they turned and saw the presence and icy stare of Ikoku fixed upon them. It was usually too late to behave. Whole classes had been taken unaware by his presence for over three or four minutes. Girls with their legs on guys' laps had been taken unaware. Numerous folks had been punished severely. Our thought: What if Ikoku suddenly came upon us? I decided to voice my misgivings. "I no sure say I wan run dis matter again."

Doro suddenly became violent. What did we mean? Why were we so scared of a human being like us? Wasn't he breathing the same air as us? What rubbish! Then … did we want to fail?

"No be human being o," I promptly pointed out. "And he fit dey anywhere now."

"He no dey—" Doro had started to yell but stopped midsentence. Because there were footsteps, slow and descending. We gathered to peep through the door. It was Imoni. He walked past us, unaware, and descended the staircase leading to the ground floor, murmuring to himself.

[Our] Time had already started.

Doro spun to us, realizing this. "If una no one do eh, I dey do. But I swear"—and he swore furiously—"Allah!"—tapping the tip of his tongue and pointing heavenward—"when I run am, if any of una beg me, I go beat shit commot e nose." He turned to Arhe. "Gimme your phone."

Arhe hesitated. I understood. It wasn't that he didn't wish or want to give Doro the phone. It was just that if Doro was caught on this foolhardy expedition he so stubbornly wanted to embark upon, he would be implicated too by reason of his phone. It was a lot like giving a robber your gun.

"I say, gimme d phone."

Like a girl, Arhe handed him his phone. Because Doro could be violent.

Sneering at our cowardice one last time, he jacked open the door, glanced left and right, bulleted past, and began to sprint up the stairs. Arhe and I looked at each other. So he was serious. His daredevil courage must have infected us, for we both called, "Doro!"

He turned, frowning. "Wetin?"

"Wait. Make we follow you."

He shrugged. "Fast. No time."

We followed.

In this last-minute plan, crisscrossed with fear, dread, and confusion, we abandoned the plan (or maybe we simply forgot) for a lookout man stationed on the second floor. The lookout, we decided as we ran up, was going to be with us on the third floor, and if anyone came, we would simply flee to the assembly hall and take whatever punishment was handed to us if we were discovered. That would be better than being caught in the office or failing. Hearts beating, minds trying to force down images of disaster, all three of us ran.

Silence. Silence pattered on by beating hearts. Chill. Chill from the AC and terrified minds. Ticking. Ticking reminding us of time and its swift passage. Slight darkness. Stacks of strewn papers. Computers. Air fresheners. Thoughts of Ikoku, not even Imoni. Our senses had been amplified beyond normal.

"Begin locate," Doro whispered. "Careful, abeg." His voice shook.

Action.

Our movements were frenetic. The papers rustled softly but swiftly in the silence. My hands were shaking as feverish teeth would chatter.

"Biology!" Arhe whispered. "I don see biology."

Doro focused and snapped. The flash lit up the room, and darkness swallowed it back. Focused and snapped. Focused. Snapped.

"English," I whispered from the other end of the table, my voice shaking with excitement and fear. "Come snap English."

Doro focused and snapped. Snapped. Turned the pages and snapped.

Ten seconds passed.

"Literature," Arhe.

"CRS," Doro. CRS broke the tension. We managed a giggle. What kind of a fool failed Christian Religious Studies?

The UPS beeped. We froze as the fluorescents flickered. So Old Man Imoni had fixed the power supply so soon? Our search intensified. All these counted for nothing if we couldn't get maths.

"Government," Arhe. "Leave objective. Snap only theory."

But Doro snapped objectives and theory and then tiptoed out to peep for the umpteenth time.

"Una neva see maths?" I asked.

Nobody had seen math. The search had become more frantic. We didn't care for care anymore. This could be our last chance. We didn't want to fail. Time was going. Imoni filled our thoughts.

"Hey, God! Where mathematics come enter nah?" Arhe cried out. I looked at him in disgust and wanted to hit him.

In the distance, we heard the faintest of footsteps. Old Man Imoni's, obviously. We had to pull out. Now. I pulled out, leaving Arhe and Doro still searching.

"Arhe! Doro!" I called frantically at the door, rushing to glance at the staircases. Old Man Imoni. "Make we dey move."

Arhe pulled out, searching as he was leaving, more unsatisfied and displeased than frightened.

"Doro!"

Doro wasn't going to leave there without seeing, at least, the objectives of the maths question papers. I couldn't leave Doro, because he was my friend. Arhe couldn't leave Doro, because Doro had his phone and could get caught. I glanced at the staircase. Imoni was already on the middle of the first flight of stairs leading to the second floor.

"Doro!" But Doro was still searching.

"Doro! Abeg, abeg make we dey pull out."

"I don see am," he said in the highest, most excited pitch of a whisper. "I don see am."

The sheaf of exam papers was heftier than the rest. Even heftier than English. That worried me even though I was excited. He focused. Snapped. Flipped and snapped. Snapped.

Imoni was already on the first flight of steps leading to us, keeping us from going down. We could clearly hear his footsteps now. "Imoni don come!" I said and ran. I didn't care anymore for Doro. Arhe neither for his phone. The both of us ran to the hall. It was a pretty long hall that had just one door at the end. We ran and then a sight froze us to ice.

The science laboratory was just after the assembly hall. There was Ikoku, his hands behind his back, just coming out of it with his catlike steps, looking straight at us and then straight past us to Doro, who was just coming out of Imoni's office.

The Miracle the Devil Gave for a Minute

The girl is standing in a dingy room in front of a cracked mirror. Her face is made up, but her mind isn't. The night before, she had called him and they'd spoken about compromise.

"I don't want to do anything today that would make me not want to look at myself in the mirror tomorrow," she had said. Her voice had been weak like she'd already made up her mind before saying that. There was a slight pause and in it a mutual chuckle that came out forced.

"You gotta do what you gotta do," he had said, sighing.

And they'd spoken about jobs, short story collections, and titles. He stared at the wall in the darkness till he cried after she hung up. She would never know this.

The week before, Blue had called her, excited and chattering. Blue told her that she was booking a flight that evening to Abuja and that she'd gotten her things ready already—the fitted skirts, the Gucci bags, the makeup kit, the UK-used iPhone X two exes had paid a good three-quarters of the price for. "I want to catch beta man o, I swear down," she'd sworn. Blue never shaded or sugarcoated her shit. That's why the girl in the dingy room loved her. So she listened, boredly observing a cockroach venture cautiously from a crack in the wall and dart to another crack, and she laughed outwardly, but she had a cave-in inwardly. Because all she'd eaten that day was a shriveled roadside chicken neck and a chocolate bar squashed in her bag, melted by the heat in her room. She didn't eat them to halt her hunger. She did to conserve what little energy she had from diminishing further. There were the short story gigs piled in her mailbox, waiting to be edited. She had to keep awake for those. These were what she was thinking about as Blue chattered on about (the) law school, (in) Abuja and (the) men (in it). In that order.

The inquiries leaped at her. "Have you gotten your things? When are you booking your own flight?"

She recoiled from the question. Lack is one of those things in life we sometimes own yet refuse to admit. Shame would have forced her to lie, but thankfully, a beeping sound that turned out to be a call from her brother cut it. She couldn't think of a lie to tell Blue, and it didn't matter that they considered themselves sisters from different misters.

"Hey, babe, can I call you back?" she said, revving urgency in her voice. "It's Amare."

"Oh, Amare. How's he?" Blue said, disappointment in her voice. "Do and comman call me fast joor. Let's go and register together. I want us to be roommates."

"I swear!" the girl swore. Then she laughed a little, hung up, and picked up Amare's call, relief quickly fading and anxiety rearing because she knew what the boy was calling for.

She exhaled to keep her voice from shaking. "Hey …"

"How're you?" Amare asked, but there was nothing in his tone to show he was interested in how she was.

"I'm fine. How're you?"

A pause. Then, "The porter told me to get out today," he replied in a tone that humiliation had turned testy. "He was shouting. People were there."

His tone. If he wasn't her brother, she would've called him an entitled little bastard, yelled at him to shut up, and hung up immediately. (She regretted thinking that.) "You'll have to wait," she said simply. "I don't have enough now."

"So I've paid school fees and I'll start going home because I cannot pay hostel fees?" Amare spat. "Waz all these ones you're saying?"

"See, I don't have money abeg," she replied, tipping over into a lower bout of resignation she had no idea existed.

"Which one is you don't have money?" Amare spat again.

There was silence before she ran mad.

"Where is your father?" Very mad. "Are you stupid in the head or something? Are you mad? Where is your father that keeps praying to his father in heaven?" Her boyfriend had never witnessed her angry. Only mildly annoyed. No one knew she could get angry. She just snapped one day and everyone darted into their cracks like that cockroach. And she had snapped into that mood now. "Don't you ever in your life talk to me like that. Are you mad? Am I your father? Won't you ask your father what he's doing with his life, allowing his children to gather to feed him?"

She shouted curses at his father, who had fasted himself into an ulcer and still spent the days serving "Trust God, he will provide" for breakfast, lunch, and dinner. She shouted his stupidity to Amare, who now was stupefiedly silent. She shouted about her selfish elder sister, who paid more attention to her own toothache than mumsi dodging a creditor, buying from more would-be creditors, and not eating for two days when there were too many creditors.

"Don't you ever—" She yanked the phone from her ear, her breath furious, her fists balled so tight she felt the pain gather and go hot through her veins up to her shoulders. Her rage made her shake. Then the WhatsApp group messages began to pour in.

"Law school resumes on Tuesday, the 19th"—Cyrus, the unbelievably short class rep.

"Make una no carry pressing iron come law school o"—Tij, a chubby little loud bat.

"Reg. go soon start—" another unknown entity with three smirking emojis for an identity.

"Where did dey post u 2?"

"A whole tw0-ninety-five grand for school fees, for dis Buhari regime?"

"Stupid Yola …"

"Lag … V.I, baby …"

Reply to "A whole two-ninety-five grand for school fees …" … "Use am collect land nah, goat."

"I'm already dere …" Another.

She swiped down, tapped the network icon, activated the silent mode, gathered her knees in her arms, and buried her head in her knees, anguish an approaching rumble, despondence a thunderclap, the stormy rain her tears. The phone rang a few minutes later, but she hadn't the strength or will to pick up. Hours later, as she curled her skinny frame around her pillow, drained and hungry, she reached for her phone. There were four missed calls, three from Blue in quick succession and one from her boyfriend. She dialed her boyfriend. The conversation was short and sparse. Then she switched off her phone and battled a headache till sleep came. Again.

Her phone glows, and a message dings. She swipes up to see Uber's "gray Corolla two minutes away" notification. She is numb, silent and staring, apprehension creeping into her about the step she is about to make and whether it will be to solve just this problem just this one time or the first of the links in the chain that just this first would form, a go-to backup plan. She is thinking about it and not liking it, and her bowels are starting to strain. Life is staring her down into this descent it has sunk her to, but she's there, in the mirror, holding on to what little defiance her dignity has clutched to.

Horns. Short pumped blasts. No doubt the Corolla. When Amare was sick six months ago, she was with her boyfriend, who'd been feigning sleep. He had heard her stand and quietly tiptoe to the passage, had heard her whispered questions and pained sighs. He had heard snatches of the conversation, surmising that there were not even enough funds to get the boy a fucking diagnosis. "So what will happen to him now?" he had heard her ask. Nothing. Because there was simply no money to do shit. She wouldn't have liked that he'd heard that, so he had kept feigning sleep. But later that day, after he had "woken up," he had looked into her eyes. They had revealed nothing but said something: a pain only she would experience, a pain only she would know of. And now, as that horn blasted, those were the eyes that stared back at her.

She worked up defiance and swept up the remnants of her dignity as she silently cursed life and reached for her bag. She stepped out of the room, turned the locks shut, and walked out, specs on, past the gate. The Corolla hummed, grayish gold in the sun. She walked to it, and the tinted windows slid down.

The driver had his teeth out, and a genuine smile. "Good afternoon, madam."

"Good afternoon."

She paused, seemed to contemplate, gave a smile the size of a shrug, opened the door, and sat.

"Where in 'Lere, sister?"

"Nassa. Behind the Pizzas."

"Oh!" He glanced at her and seemed to conclude something inwardly. "Oh."

Her heart was beating as he reached for the timer.

"Your trip starts now …" he said.

The car began to move, and her heart stopped.

Nassa was five star, one of those "toosh," tight spots in hood places. You never imagined something so covert 'posh' in a place so sordid. And that was the idea. It made the bourgeoisie feel hood-acquainted. You say you've been to Nassa and guys start to gaze at you when you're not looking and ladies start to famz.

The car rode into the streets behind the Pizzas, streets shaded by trees with overhanging branches that formed tunnels, that seemed to dictate their own measure of sunlight. In various corners kids shot rubbers; others threw slippers. The bigger age groups were gathered in impatient clusters, something looking like a bottle of crack with thinned smoke in their midst. The mallams sat silent with radios to their ears, the sport buffs stood in front of a shop that had a telly showing wrestling, and in this little world, where every man did what he could to survive till the next day, she wondered the how of the what she was getting herself into as she bumped through potholes and turns, whether all ends justified the means. Amare. Mama. Amare. Mama. Law school.

The building emerged off a sharp bend just before she began thinking about house rent. The name was written clearly on it, and the Uber man was dipping his head, trying to tell her they had arrived o, that she should not forget how she was dressed o, the big phone she was using o, and her beautiful lithe figure o … plus the tip that had to follow o.

"How much?"

He looked at the screen, "Not much. One-eight."

How thankful she was! She had budgeted ₦2,500. Okay, so she'd get a bottle of water and a handkerchief. A packet of cigarettes too, something that'd make her look bad. Nolly and Holly always said cigarettes gave bad girls a persona that attracted more money. And, sure, she wanted to get the biggest amount possible out of this so she wouldn't have to do it again.

So she handed the man ₦2,000, standing there, innocently, thoroughly believing that the taxi man wasn't even aware that there was something like a tip that existed in his line of work, not to talk of having faith in it. Mtcheeew. There he was, this driver, looking at this rich girl and thinking why on earth rich people always had to be the stingiest and why this one was waiting for ordinary ₦200 when she was going to fuck a Nassa man. And there she was, beginning to swell her face from the heat, looking around for where to get water and hanky.

Grudgingly, he gave her the change. Innocently, she asked for every inch of it, the ₦5 on top. The man was disgusted. *Well, I knew it*, he would think to himself out of spite. These girls could hang out with big guys with big cars, but they still had zero shit. Empty. Another Facebook post on why he was proud of doing what he was doing even if he was earning something little. Little but honorable. She would never know what he thought, just like he wouldn't know about Amare, Mama, house rent, and decisions.

The cigarette packet in her purse and the bottle of water hanging by the cap between her pistol pair, she dabbed at the stubborn little beads of sweat that had begun popping from her nose and forehead, counting her steps, her heart beating as she went for it, into the gate. Into the life. Past the lobby and on to the receptionist, who gave her the number of the room with a knowing, lingering half smile. She moved without thinking of anything. Winding through the spiraling staircases, glancing at the plastic plaques that said numbers next to names of African cities, she went for Ababa. She stood, taking deep breaths that helped in no big way, contemplating for a minute before rapping on it with her knuckles.

A voice emerged from the other side four series of raps later, a small, ready voice that sounded like it was sorry it hadn't replied three taps earlier. A shuffle came, the door swung open, and a fine bearded fellow wearing an extralarge T-shirt stood before her, turning a full toothpick in his mouth the way full-bellied men do. She took him in all in a glance and struggled for what to say. His smile began to emerge as his eyes roved. He began to say something vague that he somehow expected her to understand and act on. Then he called her name. "Right?"

Nothing came off her lips. She simply nodded and forced a smile. This was the 300-pound bull of a man she would fuck.

The size of the room. The brand of vodka on the table. The pendants that lay in carelessly tossed piles of shiny. The Samsung phones beside them. She took them all in. Yes, she was apprehensive because this was the first time she'd allow her body to be touched and licked and penetrated, smacked and kissed, sweated up and cuddled around for money, but even in that apprehension was a pocket of hope and contentment that she wouldn't have to do this twice, just this once. Once and for all. Why, if he had all these, generous payment wouldn't be a problem, would it? She'd calculated ₦400 grand in her head. She knew it had to be that amount. With that money, she reasoned, she'd pay the fees. She'd get herself a used HP laptop. She'd work as hard as ever in law school, studying hard, shuffling studying with writing gigs, and then she'd get a decent job and say bye to "the life." Suddenly it seemed like this bean sack of a fellow right here with a flat head and the half-drunk eyes of a dazed toad held the keys to her life. Suddenly it seemed like her future lay in how well she could please him, fuck him, slurp his cock in her mouth, sling him to heights he'd never reached. She had to be apprehensive.

His laughter jerked her out of her thoughts, the kind of laughter that grew off of big men, skippy, descend-y, lengthy. He was talking big bills over the phone—500 million, 29 million, and "I can't fly without my spaniel"—and she knew it was one of those calls where the caller simply said stuff to make the listener hear. She wasn't sure if she was being jealous or if her lack of even a speck of what he was offhandedly saying made her think that; all she was thinking about was that 400,000 naira and the best way to pretend she wasn't interested. Soon he was done.

"So what is your name?" His voice had quickly descended to that tone boys use to greet a girl after they'd greeted their gang of guys. She smiled and repeated her name. "Yours?"

"Just call me …" and he gave a title instead.

Silence reigned. She kept her eyes glued to the telly, pretending to take to the shit that was showing. He sat on his couch like a hippo in its pool, tapping at his phone, exclaiming, chuckling to himself.

"What do you even enjoy there?" he asked derisively.

"Oh, nothing," she quickly replied. So he ordered her to bring the remote and began flipping the channels every two seconds, hissing at the variety of boredom cable TV provided. And when he was tired of the silence that seemed to fall ever steeper, he waddled into the inner room and came back a few minutes later with a towel and a leer, running his tongue over his lips like a reptile. He stood right in front of her and presented his palms, which looked so white they felt leprously soft.

The swiftness of everything tumbled like a pack of cards in her mind. Now was the moment she was going to do it. She forced a smile and placed her hands in his, and he gently made her rise, battling an urge to pin a pillow against her head and hump her so hard the next man would see nothing but chewed bones to chow. Even if he was that next man.

But he said, "Just make me happy," as he kissed her on the neck (his breath smelled of poultry with unchanged sawdust), "and I'll bless you. Hmmm!" His tongue ventured slowly from his face and found the lines in her throat, and she felt her toes curl in her shoes. "Do you need a drink?" he whispered.

By God, she needed a drink. Something, anything to make her withstand and distance herself from this man that had suddenly become an ordeal.

"Just a little bit," she whispered back, settling her arms around his neck, making her eyes dreamy, and sassily picking his upper lip with hers. "I need you." Verily, verily, I say unto you, there hadn't been a worse lie recorded in history told with such a pleasant face. But this meant ₦400,000, and ₦400,000 meant the future, and ye who cast stones, would you not fuck a billionaire that smelled of poultry bedding and swear he sweated holy water and shat lilies?

He smiled broadly.

"Then let's get ourselves drunk," he whispered and spun to grab drinks.

And so they went, his hand squeezing and squashing and patting and smacking her ass as she tried a catwalk, her giggles girly, glasses to their lips as they sat on the bed, sex on one's mind, the future on the other's.

———————

All could have gone well had he not asked for one thing.

Yes, in the mild horny rage the drink had cast his mood into, he had slapped her thighs apart and fallen into that pussy like quicksand. Yes, he had poured vodka on and run his lips and tongue over every part of her body. Yes, he had sucked on her toes and she had gloomily returned the disfavor. Yes, what shriveled little stem he had for a cock, she had sucked on as a sullen child would on her thumb. Yes, she had nearly wept as he ruthlessly smacked her ass more than he humped her, doggy style, shouting at her to "grind on that mamba and give it to me, dirty black *bitch*!" Yes, he had done and said and acted on the most unprintable of unprintables his mind had mulled over. Yet, there was something she couldn't take. While she knelt, her elbows to the bed and her ass high up in the air, he had buried his face between her ass cheeks, taking deep lungfuls of what he called ass fragrance. He had spat in it, dabbing and digging a tunnel out of her anus with his lips and tongue.

"What are you doing?" she had stuttered, a little alarmed.

He mumbled something gruff that had the tone of a translation that had to be "Will you shut up!"

And she had shut up.

But it was when she felt that "mamba" caressing her ass cheeks, ready to plunge in, that she crawled as fast as her knees could and half shrieked, "I can't do anal sex o!"

In the half-light the telly cast, she could make out the aghast expression on his face. It was the rage and disbelief of a man who always got what he wanted, turned down.

"Are you mad?" he asked in a hoarse half whisper. "Am I not paying you? Are you mad?"

She could feel her tongue twist in her mouth, squirming around for words that never came. Just "I don't do anal sex."

"Den get out, you fockin bish." The angry Igbo in him had come out now. He yelled at her as she crawled out of bed. Yelled at her as she hurriedly wore her stuff. Yelled pores into her humiliation that now wore her like a skin, pores that bred and breathed. Kept yelling at her as he pulled off a portion and hurled the remainder of the crumpled bundle of naira notes at her. Pride didn't make her want to take it, but need bent her and made her pick it up. Like a slave. She left thinking about Ned Stark after his "confession" that still led to his beheading, another naked girl with clothes on walking down a street called life.

But, you see, the girl still had to pay her fees. And the girl knew the bastard who had shouted at Amare was still there, looking for another opportunity to shout again. And she knew there was Mama, who stood small and broken and helpless before her creditors. And there was the house rent. And the thousand little things she knew money could buy. She knew there was just one way to get it. She knew, even though a humiliation so great, one she couldn't bear to think of even once after that day, stalked her like a shadow. The idealistic part of her rebuked her for wanting to do something similar to what she'd done as the pragmatic part of her told her that her first experience would count for nothing if she didn't do it again and get what she expected out of it. Why on earth, it would say, would you decide to let these people continue to suffer just because you had a bad experience? Wouldn't it be a waste of the first experience if you decide not to have a second that might give you what you want? Or do you have another way?

This is what would push her ten days later to the second hotel, in front of the second door that she would nearly keep from knocking. It is what would make her rap on it and stand in front of this handsome young man no older than midtwenties, holding a cordless game pad.

It was not that his presence jarred her. It just surprised her in the kind of way that nearly curved into shock when she surmised that she was soliciting money for sex from someone who wasn't only younger than she expected but as young as her. In her mind, she cursed life. Big (but young still) with a crop of wire-tangled beards about his cool white face, he seemed like a guy who had and asserted his own sense of taste.

"Hey."

"Hi."

"You are—" and he called her name. "Right?"

"*Si.*"

His eyes shifted, and he looked behind him.

"Spanish. *Si.* I meant yes."

He laughed and told her to "come on in."

She stepped into and was run into by the battering AC. It wasn't actually a room. It was something between that and a suite. It was big. The telly didn't just hang; it was plastered to a rough oak stand, silent, replaying his FIFA game. What little sound was coming off it cocooned her, the bass gently thrumming in her from all sides, low but charged. She was trying to appear bored, used to this, but she felt herself not being able to help it, struggling to keep up with conversation, even though banal. They stayed silent and awkward for a while.

The boy said he was "Kuwait." He didn't watch her face for a reaction as people with such strange names might. He was rather watching her because he was searching for something tense. She was responding because he had the type of locks Ogulu had. She was afraid how fast she was falling for him. And he had a tattoo too on his neck, BAMN, crested gothic style. She couldn't, wouldn't, believe this was her being like this, wanting to touch him. She had imagined someone old and stocky, eager and ravenous, bizarre, rough and lewd and mocking and abusive. She had been lucky. She could start something with him. This didn't have to end with sex. He was calm, struggling to be if he wasn't, even though he had something in his eyes that darted from her every time she tried to hold his gaze. He played a song that might have been Diced Pineapples and tapped low the lights. Casually, she took a Rothmans stick and asked for a "spark" (was that as she had heard her boyfriend call it?).

"Eh?"

"Lighter?"

"Oh, ssspark—" he said, looked around, and handed her something the size of a matchbox and shimmering gold, appearing amused to watch her smoke.

She had never smoked a cigarette in her life. Her boyfriend didn't bass, just blau-d. She didn't even like the smell of dope, and she'd warned him a couple of times that she'd kill him if he ever smoked ciggies. Now, she didn't need to do this, and she knew she didn't, but see, there was something about life that violated her esteem and made her want to see how fast life could bring good tidings if you acted like what or who you weren't.

She stuck it to her lips, brought the lighter to the butt, and choked on it. His head was in his hands in an instant. He was covering his face, giggling. How cute! It was a childish, innocent giggle. He reached for them. Plus he bought a bottle of water for her. He lit. Bassed. Tried to catch snatches of smoke off the air with his lips. He bit back a choke, and he was high and moody in minutes, suddenly eager at her, like those men, to her disappointment, like that last man. He grabbed at her head and squeezed his lips on hers as she tried to adjust hers to his. He was squeezing her breasts, and although tense and unyielding at first, she responded in seconds because with this one, she didn't feel the need to pretend. It came naturally. She was pushing him down and unhooking her bra in an instant. He was squeezing her nyash, and she was already getting wet, and he was slipping her left nipple between his gap tooth. She felt proud fucking this young guy she already wished for herself. She was thinking about something ₦600,000 now. She'd be made. Fuck! He was worth it nah.

A pair of hands tightly gripped her waist now, pushing a seven-inch—expanded nineish-inch—into her, hammering her womb, denting it to a weak pulse. She felt his lovemaking proper. His hands cupped her boobs as they peaked together, as they vibrated and stayed warm in each other for half a minute before collapsing loose. They were panting heavily while he slid across the bed to the bedhead drawer for a white handkerchief.

"Shey I should clean you?" he asked, already proceeding to wipe her crotch and thighs with it. A familiar thought but one she couldn't quite place flitted past. Slight alarm registered and rose at first … It died down as he paused and appeared to wipe himself with it … and then her again. He did it in a manner that she found a little thorough—her clit and her thighs—and then he tossed the handkerchief into the drawer, giggled, cuddled with her, and kissed her forehead and then her lips.

The 30 percent of unease she felt died, and she began to yearn right there in his arms to make him love her, treat her right, and give her whatever he had to give but willingly. She felt like telling him about herself. Maybe this was the one miracle the devil could give, even for a minute. She needed this, and she needed him. She simply just needed law school and to put her future in gear and full throttle. She slept in his arms, thinking about how much he would give and what she would do with what she hoped he would give.

It came a little less than twenty-four hours later.

He started by saying he had nothing and that he was "just managing." There was a way he was saying it, like he was so that he could be doubted. Her heart sank, but she nodded and said she understood, putting herself in his arms for the morning. She didn't want to leave. She was willing to be there with him, to hear him talk whatever he had to say about himself so she could connect it somehow to herself and make conversation that would make him like her. But he never did. He just gave her a swollen envelope that could swell any ego. Into his Bentley they slipped and straight back to the junction of her cranky crib. He gave a smile and an "I'll call you. I promise." She gestured for a kiss. It felt hot and seemed passionate. The "I promise" he said sounded to her like it had no other option but to be believed.

The envelope was in a black nylon wrapped into her purse. She was still thinking of that and getting a thrill out of not letting herself wonder how much was in there. And he seemed in a hurry just as she had a vague, distant feeling that he was fleeing from something, from her. Even when he smiled brightly at her and waved, she walked back, her thoughts continuously going back to the handkerchief, concerned thoughts setting in as to why he had kept glancing at the handkerchief when it was in the drawer and whether he had actually wiped himself with it. She convinced herself that she was being paranoid for absolutely nothing. Her future was in gear. Her happiness worked up a hum she drowned her paranoia with. Life was good.

———

The doors were locked. The room was bright, but the curtains were drawn. Her ears swelled as she unwrapped the nylon and felt the raw weight of what was in her hands, what it could get, and what was hers. Hers. All this for just one round of sex! She pulled the already partitioned wads off the tightness of the overall rubber band because the sensation of dumping each pulled wad made her feel enormous. She arranged them in neat, slick, mint-smelling notes of nine. Her mind worked as her heart raced. If they were a hundred notes each … Jesus! And she was damn right sure it was a hundred notes apiece! So she began to count. And they turned out to be a hundred notes apiece. Her head exploded. Her ego … she was a millionaire! Good god!

This was a feeling she had longed to experience a long time ago, the day she'd earn her first million, how she'd have earned it. It suddenly seemed like she'd been wasting her time doing gigs (even though she immediately regretted thinking that). She would just have done this when they were kicked out of their fourth and fifth houses, to put food on the family's table, to set up something. She could meet someone big if she stepped up her game, because she had class, and she'd use the money from what she did to get done what she loved, and then step out clean of the game. But isn't this what they all said, she reminded herself and turned the edges of her lips down in response.

Her phone rang. It was her boyfriend. She picked up, and he noticed her voice, happy. Instantly, like one of those revelations that can't lie, he knew she had fucked someone. He had had a dream about it, and he didn't normally believe dreams but that one he did believe. It was clear she had, he reasoned, and when he confronted her about it and insisted on making and growing a persistent pest off of it, she just dropped silent (just because she truly respected him) … at least until he was tired and pissed and cursing, ending it with a rude hang-up. Sadness, like an anchor, would weigh on his heart. But in this life, as he would remind himself, the poor had no fucking say. Disagreeing with this made him a fool, and he knew that was one more thing he didn't want to be. If you no get money, baba, lost your smelling face!

It was a few days later that they spoke, in the afternoon. He picked up as soon as she called back. She was fine. Her voice was fine. He was mad she was fine, and he was increasingly exhibiting the features of enemies of progress, but she sidestepped his ignorance ever so glibly. But she was still that same old girl, even when he knew she had much more. They weren't dating-dating anymore, but she still deeply fucking cared for him, even though she didn't necessarily care if he left for long periods of time just because he felt like being a tantrum-throwing spiteful yam head. She told him everyone was fine, that everyone was really fine.

"Where are you?" she asked.

He was still staying with his brother, sweeping his brother's parlor, but he would be traveling for a church convention on Thursday.

"Oh."

He noticed voices in the background. "Where are you? Who's talking?"

"Abujaaa and a dick from my class."

"From your class! Law school?"

"Oh yeah."

That jarred him. For some reason he'd never thought about it, that she'd have gotten enough to actually leave for law school (even though he had it somewhere at the back of his mind that she could).

"Wow!"

"Wow what?"

"You're in law school is all. How's law school?"

"Law school's fiiine," she said with the kind of glee tinged with regret.

He was glad for her, but there was something small in him that insisted on being sad and envious enough to cut her off when she started to talk about it.

The brief silence puffed itself huge, and she pierced it. "I saw you on my 'People You May Know' section. You've activated."

He sighed. "Oh, that? Yeah. Same old stupid people."

"You should just go back to hibernation," she countered, always hurt when insults were directed to a group where a person she liked was.

"Same old stupid people," he repeated to annoy her.

She said nothing. Arguing with him was exhausting.

Now that he had gotten her mad, he would continue. "Imagine the nonsense the other day … Someone in my youth church tagged me to it … This guy came for deliverance to our branch, and he said he was in deep shit and that he'd come to the end of the line."

She kept silent. He would continue. He always did. He did. "He'd done shit. Now payback time had come. Guy said he was tired of picking $200 every half once in a while, that that was lame shit. He said he wanted more. He met a baba in the west, and the old juju man gave him handkerchiefs to clean girls he'd fucked. That's the g-plus they do? They just fuck girls and clean up their toto, getting more money from the 'soiled' handkerchiefs? He confessed to the pastor that all these girls now walk about empty, with empty destinies and futures." He paused. Derision made his tone venomous. "This is what educated people are carrying on their time lines when the Boko haram boys are wasting hundreds of our soldiers?" He was hissing now. He grew more pissed the more he spoke. He was, sadly, one of those idealists who always had solutions but never solved anything. This was one of the things that irritated her about him. One of those people who had an idea about what was wrong with the world and how to solve it but still sat on his ass for all the effort he could make in exchange for all the change he wanted to see.

He was still ranting. "This is the kind of news our youths of today are carrying? Seriously?"

But her mind began to rove shortly after. It halted, reversed, and went through what she had just heard him say. She found out this was something she didn't like.

Her voice was of neither extremes as she asked what he had just said. If he caught the slightest note of inquiry in her tone, he would definitely ask her why she was asking and subsequently refuse to repeat what he'd just said. He might even go as far as connecting the dots because he had a talent for fishing out everything that wasn't in his interest.

"What did you say," she said, "about the fucking and the handkerchiefs?"

"Yeah. Can you imagine the fantastically stupendous heights of trash …"

But she wasn't even interested in any of what he imagined at that moment.

She cut him short and asked him again to talk "about the fucking and handkerchiefs." He paused. Her heart skipped. The stupid, curious bastard was at it again. He had caught something off her tone.

"Why are you asking?" Then his tone dropped mischievously. "Or did you fuck someone who cleaned your pussy thereafter with a white handkerchief?"

She hated him exceedingly then, but she needed to hear what he had to say. "No," she said firmly. "I'm just asking."

"I don't believe you're just asking," he insisted stubbornly.

"Okay."

"I said guys take a handkerchief and clean up the pussies of the girls they've finished fucking. They take this handkerchief to the juju baba, who uses it for rituals for more money, at the expense of the girls, apparently. That is just stupid. How can pussy juice make anyone rich?"

There was silence. He noticed an even steeper silence than she'd displayed prior, and he had no idea why. The pause lingered. She remembered their conversation the morning that had started this story. She remembered that question she'd said she'd ask herself. She remembered the night she fucked the guy with the Bentley. She remembered him, his eyes, the heftiness of his payment. There was a time when she never believed all this nonsense and would have laughed it off. Now, this wasn't that time to disbelieve, especially when it was happening to her. The time span of the miracle the devil had given—that minute—was up all of a sudden.

Bananas

It is a hot day and I am waiting, sitting on a friend's doorsteps, momentarily snapped out of boredom watching a super bizarre spectacle of two male dogs, the brown one's leg deeply lodged in the black one's butthole. These evil beasts, in their silence, are struggling to pull themselves apart like someone fixed them like that in the first place. How did it happen? How do these things happen? End time signs, I conclude as I cast about for a stick or a stone to strike or hurl at these abominable canines. I finally find something sizable enough to inflict hurt, and they, these shameless tempters of God's wrath, flee farther than the fuel of my own wrath can take me, paw still in ass, of course. End time signs!

So while I'm there, a lady, my friend's neighbor, approaches yelling a song. She's just from the market, I can tell, with all these sacks and bags emitting a confluence of smells best described as fishy. The horridly stinking type. She's got her toddler strapped to her back, some chubby, sleek-black creature of a boy I've always known to be intent on being noisy and implacable.

"Hey, Taribo! You don come?" she yells at me, and I bow my head. "You no go help me carry my bag?"

I force back an eye roll much the way I force the smile I'm now wearing as I rise and ease a bag out of her hand.

"It is indeed I," I greet her. "You are not seeing a ghost. It's me Taribo, King of the West."

She attempts to grab and pinch me for my sarcasm, but I skip out of reach, not because I'm in the mood to play but because I don't feel like being the human that has to smell like dead fish. I ask about the market, whether she bought "rubber" for me, and she tells me my mind is an army of maggots. "I'm tired," she announces as she unlocks the gate. She has to cook for her husband. This is what marriage does, she says, hissing and slumping into a sofa. The toddler kicks. It's funny, this woman! Every time she complains, she goes on to do what she grouched about. That's why I laugh when she drags herself up, loosens her wrappa to let the toddler down, and grumbles all the way to the kitchen. This is what marriage does.

"Help me look Atie for me," she calls from the kitchen because she knows it'll be too late for me to stutter and give excuses.

This task, I'm just so fucking terrified of it. I've never held a baby, and I won't like to start with this one.

The fan is turning, creaking, powerless before stuffiness. Here I am, fucking hungry, tasked with attending to a known troublemaking toddler. But what can I do? There's just the both of us in this cramped room, him an arm's length away from me, pots and metal clanging from the kitchen, making my teeth rattle. I stare at him the way a wife would stare at a single lady smiling at her husband. His oval face is caught in an expression of silent distrust. His fists are bunched. He observes me for a while and decides he can't fuck with this strong sun-charred face staring right into his. I can see fright start to creep into him: his eyes are starting to falter and his mouth is starting to mutter "scared" in baby language.

I snap at him with my fingers, and taken aback, he shuts himself into silence. But just for a bit. He's got demons, and right now, they're charging him into displaying the mischief. His lips are starting to crumple at the edges. I snap at him again, clapping my hands in his face and pushing a warning finger in his forehead, but his demons are stronger than me. His mouth is already wide open. He's burst into a cry, it's volume without preamble or progression, so loud that it startles me. It angers me the most that he has destroyed the silence, that he has added his toddler madness to the heat. I glare. Little motherfucker doesn't care. I glance at the passage to make sure his mother isn't peeping. She's not, so I slam a palm over his mouth and the back of his head at the same time, shaking him back and forth. This maddens the fuck out of him, and the ceiling nearly crashes down on us when his mouth finally finds sound.

"Atieeee, wetin dey happen ooo," his mother calls from the kitchen.

Ah, so she's still there, and she's expecting me to take care of her goblin, eh? Okay. So I make threatening faces and forehead him, determined to make him as miserable as he's making me. This one has no shame. He just keeps crying louder and louder, and it is only when I hear his momma running down that I dump him on my laps and show gestures of concern so fake I fear she'll see through.

"Wetin dey worry am?" she says, snatching him from my lap and trying to palliate the overpampered, fatheaded, lil' elephant. Now he's gotten attention. So he cries louder, and this is the point I just want to exclaim, "Take me, Lord!" and mean it. But I say I don't even know what's worrying him, that he suddenly started crying, probably because he doesn't like my face. So she's starting to stare at me to see if there's something guilty about my face, but I'm staring at the boy to avoid her stare. Because if she does stare close enough, she'll see that I'm dead guilty. But is that even my fault?

"Maybe he dey hungry."

I seize at the suggestion and nod my agreement.

"He dey even suck he thumb."

"Ah!"

She dumps the baby in my arms and tells me, "I dey come." So I'm forced into the company of this furious little guy once again. A few seconds later, she bounces back holding a small bottle.

"My things for pot dey burn. I dey come. Feed am." And she thrusts the bottle into my hands, leaving me standing, stunned at her nonchalant assumption of what has now become my job. I sit, my face a deadly frown, the toddler screaming, the mother yelling— all of these the results of this creature I'm supposed to pacify with this ... Wait, what is this? I raise the bottle to eye level and observe its contents, swirling it slowly. It's cloudy, seedy, not at all something that looks like what kids could grow on, even if it was thrice richer. But I shrug, and because I want this toddler to shut the fuck up and silence restored, I put what is remaining of my hope into that bottle and stick it into his mouth. Immediately, he grabs at it and locates the bottle's nipple in an instant with eager lips, gurgling, hiccupping on his greed. He coughs a couple of times and sucks hurriedly and, after a while, contentedly and silently.

It is a wonder the things that fix much bigger things. David fixing Goliath. Israel fixing Egypt, Jordan, and Syria. This weird-looking liquid fixing this kid. It must be a wonder then, whatever this is, I think to myself. I try to take a closer look, but the toddler, surprisingly, holds greedily onto it, imploring me with his eyes to give it back each time I mischievously slip it from his lips. Little by little, the contents deplete. Ah! I should taste what a miracle this is, I think, shouldn't I? I observe it closely once more in the hopes of nursing a thought strong enough to counter and dissuade me from acting out the thought I'm already intent on. There's no such thought.

I look left and right. The silence is there; the mother is not. I shake the contents of the bottle, raise it to my lips, give it a fleeting thought, and say, "Fuck it," and then suckle a mouthful. Nothing hits me, but soon, just as I swallow, I feel the 'taste.' It is tasteless, awful in its tastelessness, cloudy and thickly trudging in its texture and simply a fuck's worth of an effort to try out. What in the holy hell does the kid enjoy in this? What pacifier is strong enough to have put this kid to silence and now sleep?

A quarter of an hour passes before his mother bounces in, sheathed in sweat, fanning herself with her hands.

"Ah! He don sleep?" she says, smiling contentedly.

"Yes."

"He like you o. Abi na d food?"

"He no like me. E be like say na d food."

She glances at me. I see a twinkle the size of color bright in her eyes, like she's just discovered the confirmation of something long sought.

"What?" I ask.

Her young face breaks into a full smile, and she begins to tell me, "I dey always talk am. All dis baby food no strong rish God-given breast milk."

My ears prick at the words, and my heartbeat skips and stops.

"Yes. Na breast milk dey make am grow, dey make am sleep well."

I stare at the bottle and then at the sleeping toddler. I search inside myself and find an upsurge of disgust that rumbles in and spills out of me.

"Taribo!"

I'm woken out of my thoughts and stare at her.

"Wetin dey do you? Why your face change?"

"Na your milk dey inside?" I reply.

She tries to make the connection, and when she finally does, bursts into laughter, at least, till the moment I crumble and smash a nearby stool apart with the back of my head.

How the Cock Came to Be

E get dis ebelebo tree wey dey our back hostel. When night rish, all dese ones wey feel say dem dey wise, wey feel say na deir duty to ginger d world, wey feel say dem fit jus crow anytime and anyhow for night, all of dem go show. 3 of dem. First, dem go round d tree, dey observe on a low. Next, one of dem, d red one among them gan gan, go fly rish up, dey observe, den after that, e go signal d 2 others make dem show. Dem 2 wey dey d down go follow am fly rish up too, dey till day break. When night rish, dem go start again.

You see eh, since I enter 100 level, I don dey sha OBS dis guys sha. Christmas go rish, nobody dey kpoof dem. Dem go waka dey carry shoulder. New year go reach, nobody go kpoof dem. Independence, even Children's day, nobody dey gree kpoof dem. If na dog or cat, we go understand say hungry fit dey o, but we no fit just kpoof dem. But fowl? Fawo? No nah.

So New Year rish, I no fit fall in house unto say one or two. Na d 3rd year I neva fit fall in unto say, like I talk, one or two. I jus dey, but chow no dey! Buhari regime condition all man.

Evening rish, as me and my guy Asari jus quiet, dey kpo, one of d fowl wey be like who wan prove point stroll pass. Yankee people say great minds dey tink alike, abi? No lele. I swear, me and Asari great die! As we look awaself we jus know say e go sup dah night. Hungry no fit dey dagger me when one walking feast dey stroll, baba. Y exactly we go use spit tey wash hand when sea cross leg dey chill for awa front? Na y we go dey curse bad boy Bubu for lack of food when Jehovah Jireh dey update us say make me sharpen eye?

Night rish.

As usual, d 1ˢᵗ fowl show, d red one. E observe, round d tree, fly go top. E alert e 2 brodas for d down. Dem fly go too. Asari no dey ever dull! Ijaw boy wey no get joy! Na once e follow up, climb tree, snuff am sharperly (in case d fowl by mistake get owner), hide am. Na so 2 oda fowl jus dey observe am. Me, I know say fowl get night blindness normally, but eh, fowl still dey comport for night like say nuttin' dey sup too? I no jus too reason am.

We enta house, pull e head wit' hand, boil water, soak am, commot all e feda. We add everytin wey we feel say go make am legit. Salt, sugar, water leaf, small saccharine. Na fowl we wan chop, no be ba-b-Q.

E get one tin wey Asari dey do wey I no dey ever vibe to: Eating from pot. E dey call am "testing" but really, na long throat dey worry dah fool. No be really fool sha (for may he rest in peace now). Asari stretch hand commot one piece of meat. Chew. Chow. When I look e face, I know say everywhere good, say awa new year set las las, say d fowl mye-mye.

I ask am, "How e be?"

E open e mout wan talk but na fowl language fall out. You know, I fes bust laugh because d guyman copy d sound well. Like, na full blast fowl language.

I ask again, "How e be nah?"

Baba do am again. I bust laugh, but then, I come begin OBS am well. Baba dey touch e throat small small, dey massage am, dey try cough, clear am. E be like who dey tensh. E no be like who dey joke. Na once my prick shrink na!

I call am. "Asari!"

E dey look me, begin dey spread hand like feda.

"Asari!"

Baba begin dey flex shoulder like fowl wey wan fly rish top.

By dis time, I don begin dey near door, dey scream e name.

"Asarii! Asarii, stop na!"

Baba begin crow.

Boyo, I say when I begin zab eh, I no look back. As I dey tear enter street, pass awa gate, pass under d tree, sometin say make I look up. I swear, na d oda 2 fowl I see. Dem jus dey observe me. Deir feda dey under deir chin, dem jus dey nod head, dey smile big smile.

The Rules of Withdrawal

With most banks in Naija come specific tags, most true, a few not necessarily untrue.

Zanit is notable for its crispness: The cashiers, the cash they count, the conditioning—the whole kit and caboodle. Gee Trust are a corporately branded band of bandits. Bandits of the basest pecking order. As for Echo, bro, they house the rudest, tardiest, most unprofessional sleazebags ever put in suits (the kind of sleazebags that snap at you, that hang up your call, that deduct indiscriminately from your account, and send you back to the ATM. Your task? To tell the exact words it told when it debited you). Fest Bank cannot possibly be a place any sane man would want to be on a Friday, or on a Monday either (for it is a congregation of all society's class). The Diamonds in the Rough could be swift in service (and boy do I love staring at their slick females with their tight, jutting little asses), except with the issuance of ATM cards. Hairy Tage Bank has the most bizarre, frequently recurrent excuses ever ("Oh, our national area father hasn't paid for subscription; that's why our network is bad." Or, "Oh, our bullion van's tire is flat. That's why there's no cash yet." Or, "Oh, there's no ink in our photocopying machine; that's why we don't have sufficient payment slips.") And You-Neon

Bank, oh! You-Neon Bank, in addition to their jealously guarded reputation of hardly never sharing ancient buildings with another, they have yet another reputation: having roadside welders construct their ATMs, hence the creaky, clumsy nature, which brings us to our story.

So I arrive at this You-Neon Bank ATM stand where everyone's face is creased in frustration, disgust, irritation, or downright anger. The queue is long. The sun is harsh; there is no shade from it, no respite. The security man is saying, "Wehkum to You-Non Bank. Hope ya ejjoyin awa mobye app." The door is a laboring mule, creaking open and grinding shut. Down here, on this stand, cocooned in their own world of their own anger, no one wants to talk to anyone. Why? Because, of the three monstrosities masquerading as machines, none but one is paying, handing out cash with the clumsy slowness of a man with the palsy.

"Good afternoon o. Are you the last person?"

"You are now the last person," she grunts.

Smart-ass.

"I greet o, baba! Na you be las person?"

He gives a ghost of a nod.

"Abeg, I dey your back—"

"I no dey all dose ones o. Stay your line abeg." And another lets loose a wild, indignant litany.

Grumpy ass.

"Braa, weh done o. D ATM machine dey pay money?"

"No. We just stand line to transfer card."

Sarcastic ass.

"Good afturoon, ix it poxxibull for yhu tew axxixt me wit my transaxxion?"

76

He glances at her up and down and nods.
Silent ass.

There are certain unwritten rules you must adhere to when you
want to withdraw, especially in a hostile environment like Nigeria,
where you have to apologize before you make a request—the
environment where I now find myself.

- Do not try to withdraw with more than one card (for
  someone has given you that card, regardless of whether
  it's your name written on it).
- Do not for a moment take your eyes off the machine (for
  an averted gaze is a distraction, and the ire of the crowd
  shall spill volcanic on you).
- Do not come to check your account balance, transfer,
  or recharge your phone (for you are a time waster, a
  mischievous pauper and a people displeaser).
- Do not start asking for help only when you've started
  operating the machine (for you are a time-splurging idiot).
- Do not try your card more than once (for the ATM will—
  no, must—say, "Out of Service," and the wrath of the
  people shall rain down on you like confetti).
- Do not withdraw as much as you want (for a heartless man
  will ultimately not be shown mercy).
- Do not allow any sob story cajole you into giving someone
  space (for your stupidity has automatically knocked me
  back and the ones before me).
- Do not just stand in one place like a mumu when the
  person before you moves ahead (for there's an illusion of
  movement when we do).

"This is the problem with Nigeria," one balding man is grumbling, bending forward and backward. "You see people in the line that have been waiting for four, five hours. You still want to collect all the money in the ATM machine."

"ATM," someone corrects from behind.

But he neither takes the correction nor has told us the problem with Nigeria yet. And he probably doesn't know that the withdrawer is not required by law or morality to give a shit about others as long as his card is in. Why, if others were so intent on collecting their money, they should have beaten him to it.

Resentment has started simmering and spreading along the queue. But the withdrawer is oblivious to the hissing, the silent curses, the pleading, and the occasional warning. His shoulders are squared in what could be arrogance. He lets the other hand, the one holding the money, hang down. Why shouldn't the crowd see his money?

"Your life savings nai you use take dey buga!" one person shouts, and the crowd laughs in derisive solidarity.

₦150K later, in gross violation of the sixth rule, he goes on to try to violate the first, and the crowd's ire is sparked. One self-appointed, presumptuous whippersnapper bounces forward, trying to prevent him from slotting a second card in, and a particularly audacious one tries to seize his card.

"This is the problem with Nigeria! The problem with Nigeria!" the balding man is still saying, jumping up and down in one spot.

The security man repeating his mantra is jolted out of his monotony, his face instantly animated. The withdrawer is yelling, asserting his rights, but his rights in the face of the crowd's sentiments and ire are beaten down small. But the withdrawer refuses to give in. The argument, hot and boiling, balloons into a shove, and a security officer with a baton and a barrel belly bustles forward.

"Ha! Wetin dey happen for hia?" he yells, coming between the fighters with both arms outstretched. Okay, now we've got a barrel with arms trying to calm us down?

One against many. Reason against sentimental ire. An open courthouse, the proceedings so rowdy it appears the winners are the ones with the widest vocal cords.

"Make I see your card," the security man says.

The withdrawer shows his card, breathing like he needs another pair of lungs.

The security man inspects the card front and back and then inspects the withdrawer's face like cards suddenly have passports on them. Like he can decipher the true owner of a card through the scrutiny of the visage of the withdrawer.

And then a most idiotic question he probably learned from his police father: "Na your card?"

"Yes." Ofuckingcourse!

"Err … Oya, wetin be your name?"

The withdrawer tells his name, the bank's name, and what sounds like the first three digits of the ATM number.

The security man turns to all and calms everyone down with this gesture of importance that has, no doubt, always been foreign to him. His verdict: He can withdraw his cash. It is his card as far as I can see.

So the man withdraws, and the hissing, curses, and jeers continue, but what the fuck is his business? There are iron pillars everywhere upon which anyone dissatisfied can crack any open. Plus, he has made the ATM three hundred g's less, and even better, he has won this battle against haters. He bounces off jauntily. Dababy has nothing on this one!

A huge beardless man walks directly to the young man who is in two minds on violating the seventh rule. He calmly inserts himself between the young man and a lash-batting lady, and says aloud, looking right into his eyes, "If you allow this woman"—he jerks a thumb at the lady—"take the space in front of you, I will pick you and throw you over that fence." His arms point at the fence he intends to throw the man over. Quite a fence!

His voice is stentorian, his words crisp as Zanit cash. The crowd hails him as he walks back, but he ignores everyone, for acknowledging them with a gesture of sorts or a word too many would stand the risk of watering down the effect of his intent in some way. The young man is visibly embarrassed. In private, he would have cowered and slunk. But this is public, and the worst place to stab an ego is in public. He turns, appears to consider his size (he is five foot eleven), considers the man's size (he is six foot six), and utters a half-hearted, "Wetin you mean?"

The crowd starts to mumble. The sketchiest of tensions arise. A small woman from the queue instantly asks mockingly, "Wetin be wetin e mean? You deaf, abi you die when e talk am?"

The crowd laughs. The knife in his ego is twisted, and he looks like he wants to crumple and die right there at the feet of the lady to whom he's supposed to be lending a hand, or space. That small woman is his match, his one redemptive chance to strike back. So he walks to her and starts a warning, shaking his finger at her. The woman stays silent and ignores him, and this young man with his plans foiled, decides to brave it.

He walks up to the huge man and repeats, "Wetin you mean?" But the man ignores him as a lion would a praying mantis. "Una dey wan dey use size dey show unasef. Come troway me over the fence nah." And he turns to walk back to his spot, unsure of the huge man's calm silence but determined to bandage his ego. He collects the lash-batting lady's card and folds his arms while the crowd grumbles, complains loudly, ultimately deciding to opt for the showdown between him and the Goliath who has promised to represent them.

The two men before the young man withdraw, and he climbs the steps, ready to slot in either of the cards in his hand. The card is already in when the Goliath starts to move. A mumble sweeps through the crowd. The young man, noticing, glances back and sees his nemesis, while the lady he's supposed to be helping stylishly disappears. Anyone can see that two thousand things are swamping his mind: Does he run? Does he quickly punch his password? Does he negotiate? Does he stand back and fight? Does he—

The Goliath increases his strides and grabs him by the waist of his trousers and the scruff of his neck. Everything that happens next is like a movie. Everybody's eyes go uuuuuuuup as he hurtles through air and come dooooooooown as he lands a few feet away.

The queue is no more a queue. It is a screaming, stylishly absconding group of witnesses to a potential homicide. The huge man pays no mind. He flips out his wallet, flings the already spit-out card of the thrown man far away, and slots in his. He withdraws his cash, counts it as if to make sure and walks away, deliberately stepping over the immobile human mass.

"Na army," I hear people whisper. "Na army man."

———————

Close to ten minutes pass. The queue is a queue once again, only this time much longer, with the sun blazing harsher. The machine is still creaking and clumsy. People are marveling at and talking excitedly about the events of ten minutes past, explaining the happening to newcomers, pointing farther than where the boy was thrown. This is how legends are made. The overembellishment of truth. The mystery lady is nowhere to be seen, and her young man savior has slunk off like a whipped dog.

A guy no more than twenty walks in. Small in stature, his steps are clipped, those of the shady and naturally impatient. He walks directly to the forefront, and the crowd, suspecting his intentions, shouts him down, but he pays them no mind. There is no way for him and he recognizes it. He glances at the second ATM and then the third. Hesitant, he moves to the second, peers right into it, and randomly punching whatever his fingers punch, slots in his card.

"E be like say you wan make dem seize your card!" one half warns, half mocks from the queue.

"So all of us wey stand here na fool abi?" another calls.

He keeps on at what he is doing, like the people yelling at him are no more than bleating goats helplessly restricted to a barn.

"Maybe e wan recharge card. Una no go leave am?"

So they "leave" him. He's soon forgotten. Half a minute later, he turns and descends the steps, smiling to himself. There is something ironic, almost mocking, about that smile. I leave my spot and go straight to him. He communicates something with his eyes, and with my heart beating fast, I go straight to the second machine. I can feel the insanely long queue's eyes boring holes in my back. I slot in my card. I punch in my digits. I choose my account. I wait an unbearably long time as the welded monstrosity does its thing. Then … I hear a flutter of cash. My heart literally stops. Jesus! The dispenser slips open. The 5 grand I've been waiting longer than an hour and a quarter for shoots out. I grab it and turn, and as I walk down the steps, cash splayed in my raised hand, I wink and shrug. "E dey pay ooo!"

My memory of that place is a stampede so wild it would've crushed me if I hadn't the sense to give space before the announcement.

A Once-Beautiful Dress

A confluence of colors, of pink and white, of cream and purple, and of black and yellow, wrappas and laces and dresses surround her in mounds of colored little hills. These are ma's, beautiful, just the way she learned ma was. Now she smiles, sparing herself a moment to think about ma, who the woman was, who the woman could have been now. That half smile pales because thinking about mumsi brings a crushing sense of shame to her. This is because, for as far back as her memory can go, it's been communicated to her that she, only she, was responsible for why ma died "like a fowl". Now, sitting in the middle, she puts her imagination to use, she tried to capture the radiance of ma's life through smiles. There are a few pictures she's seen of her. She'll use that.

People have frequently told her she smiles like the woman. She's seldom taken that as a compliment. Now, she does, even if a little bit.

The dress she's holding! Her melancholy spirals into a vapor. She ups her fragile frame, she jumps and lands with dainty grace, she shakes the dress in the air. Unzips it. Steps into it. Wriggles into it. Feels herself filling it, owning it.

Pregnant pause. The flimsy curtains are filtering the early sunlight into a most purified puddle that she now steps into.

She takes in lungfuls of air and exhales slowly between each. It is one thing to own something; it is another to know you do. She owns life, is filled with it, and yes, she knows she is. She moves to the front of the full-length mirror, shock and awe ballooning in her. She struggles to believe that the figure in the mirror, gazing back at her with matching awe, is actually her. She's struck by the starved-lover fierceness with which the dress hugs her newly formed curves, like it was painted there. Perhaps she'd taken no notice of herself prior to now. She doesn't know; neither does she bother to reflect or care. Right now, she's a lithe, flawless goddess.

She keeps staring, revelling in the beauty of it to the point that she feels like actually swallowing the dress. Being the dress. Beautiful. Gorgeous. She's beautiful at sixteen. Gorgeous as a lady. Ecstasy swells beneath that part of the chest people think the mind is. She works up a song and hums, accompanying it with slow tilts of the head and barely noticeable steps. She half twirls to the left. Stops. Half twirls to the right. Pauses. Her slender hands flail, in them the lazy grace of jelly, falling to the flared bottom of the dress and nimbly picking it up. Twirling and moving faster, she spins like a ballet dancer. Euphoria is what this feels like. She doesn't care that she's alone in the world anymore or that what father she has is a total stranger to her. That he's a drunken, brash brute of a humanimal with temper issues. She doesn't care that he hates her with a passion so severe and unsubtle it's almost tangible. Doesn't care that he thinks she killed her ma in childbirth. For now, it's just her, her curves, her happiness, and her beautiful dress. She feels like a woman. Do you think it's easy to be whole at sixteen?

Then she hears it.

The outer door just slammed shut.

She stops, shaken, panic stiffening her, too wrapped up in a thick black blank to think. It takes a little more than an eternal quarter minute before the swift-swirling blankness around her thoughts begins to lift and clear, leaving only panic for her to contend with. Oh no! No! No! He can't be back! It's way too early! How long has she been there? An hour? How long has she allowed foolishness for discretion? Two hours? No! He cannot see her there. There will be pain—and a lot of it—if he does. She tries to move, but she can't. Her legs seem fastened at the knees and ankles with hefty lead. There's no cloud nine anymore, just a rush of something thick and smoky coursing through her chest and thawing into hot liquid over her tongue.

She remembers the look he wore when he told her to stay away from his wife's—ma's—room. "Evil witch," he had bawled at her and shot a chopping smack to her stomach. Do not ever come here! An aching emptiness had expanded in her bowels, and she had gone nigh unconscious. He'd reluctantly taken her to the hospital, paid the bills, and left promptly. She isn't ready to experience that or anything in vague comparison to it again.

Then bloody move, she urges herself. But she can't. Her inability to both surprises and terrifies her. He'll kill you, an inner voice laden with urgency whispers, trying to galvanize her.

Fucking move!

No. She can't.

The footsteps approach, leisurely, heels brushing, scraping against the floor. Accompanied by the blend of an occasional roar and a whistle too merry she can infer the sound to be coming from a person who has drunk a glass or two too many or smoked a stick or two above the limit.

The hammering of her heart makes her chest hurt. Her breath stops. He terrifies the living daylights out of her. This man with whom nature has paired her as father. He's the stuff bogeymen are made of. The steps draw closer. She silently expels a load of breath through her mouth, not just because she is running out of air but also because she's scared he'll hear her if she breathes through her nose.

He mumbles something in a slur of a whisper. Silence. He mutters and then crowns it with a yell, the sound of an unearthly nature. Perhaps it is her name. Perhaps it is an annoyed curse or an obscenity, as he is wont to spew. She cannot say for sure. She has only just realized that a vast part of her hearing has become lost to fear. There is a violent smash-up, the sound of something toppling and crashing down in a heap. A thin, irritated grunt. Pained whimpers. Steps struggling and shuffling. Her gaze strays to the space between the door and the floor. She catches the shadows of his feet, the hesitance in them. He might be aware of the presence of someone in there.

Silence.

Longer silence.

Her gaze moves to the door itself. Now, the rhythm of her heartbeat slows down, reduced to the pace of the twisting doorknob turned in a half circle. *Cliiick!* The door's catch punctuates the silence. The plaintive whine of its hinges is a ghost in a shanty town.

Through the little space he has created, he eases in headfirst like he's wary of the unknown lurking beyond. He steps in fully. Her glance moves to his face. The hell in his hardened eyes stops her cold. He pauses. Tenderly dabs at the side of his mouth with the back of his wrist. Looks at her startlingly like he's just seen her, bushy brows risen and touching. Rage slowly substitutes for disbelief. He starts to walk toward her in a way too calm to match the fiery spectacle of hate in his eyes. She rears back without knowing it, her nerves tingling, chills rolling, feet numb against tiles.

Her back is against the wall now and unconsciously, she tries grinding herself into it to get away from him. To put as much space between them as it would allow. He moves toward her within stalking speed until he's an inch from her. All she can do now is stare down at the floor.

From a pore pops perspiration. It crawls down her forehead, dribbles its way to the side of her eye, makes a twist to her jaw, and snakes rapidly to her chin. It hangs there. His eyes move. It pleases him to see the sensation of terror he has inspired.

From the corner of her eye, she sees his hand rise from his side, and her breath skips … pausing in the suspense. Does he want to touch …? Their bodies never touched save in violence, so it's only natural that she's expecting a scream and a smack. Her body goes taut in defence. The sweat drops. The drop blurs under her gaze and seems merge into the floor. But she's still alert, aware of the potential of the horror before her.

He does none of those things. Instead, he touches her cheek with toad-cold thumbs making her flinch, making her lips crumple in distaste, making her breath hold and her fingers snap away softly in disgust. She feels his touch wander, almost lovingly, to her dress. Ma's dress. He feels the hem like he is trying to make out the texture. Then he begins to tug at it. He traces the flowers imprinted on the dress like he's drawing some sort of dark power from them.

"So alike," he whispers with a smile, a hint of deadliness in it. She feels an odd change come over him. His palms cup her face. She struggles to contain her brimming disgust. She can't speak. She dares not. She remembers the last time she did. The vicious bruise to her lips she quickly earned. The split tooth that nearly fell off at its roots.

His hands move to her scalp and he begins to hum a tone. He pulls her tresses lovingly, twirling them around his middle finger.

He tilts his head from side to side to a rhythm not in tandem with the tone he hums.

Suddenly, it happens.

His hands snatch off her head like he's touched a live wire. He smacks his palm with an inhumane force against her temple. *Tttawaiii!* Palm on skin is loud and clear as that *kpai*-sounding pop of a pricked balloon. She staggers, gripping her head with both hands, and loses her bearing in a tangle of feet, landing on the floor with a thud othat grabs her into its blackness. She thrashes herself back into the dim glow of her consciousness, too struck to feel the pain, too shaken to realize what has just happens. It bursts without preamble, shooting through every crevice of her upper body, all the way down to her toes, and then back up with a speed as swift as it is sickening; the kind of pain so terrible it reminds her of how alive she is, the way she screams.

He gets astride her as she continues to scream. Her word hole irritates him immeasurably. He smacks her across the mouth as she cowers helplessly farther into the ground, seeking refuge. The force of the strike sends blood spurting through her nostrils. He strikes again, harder this time. She feels her mouth take blood the taste of rust, the taste of fear, her fear. He rises, her along with him, and tosses her down. Her fragile body slamming, rattles the floor tiles.. Ma is on her mind. Ma's face flashes. Was this what she faced? It is with rude shock she realizes what her father is doing; that he is sprawled atop her; that he is panting, groaning, and grunting, feeling and searching; like a beast, clawing and ripping the neckline of ma's dress, making the metal buttons fly off. She struggles through her pain to process what in the hell is going on, but she can't because her mind is in too much turmoil to act as she wants it to. The bad realization dawns on her.

Oh my God! No! No, it can't be!

Gathering might, she screams as loud as she can even when it cuts and hurts like shards of glass scattered in her throat. He's still ripping, pounding through her obstinate knuckles and prying the dress from her tightly shut fists. She can't let this happen. She can't let her gift, her pride, her womanhood be snatched so easily. Her throat can hurt, but by God, she won't let that happen. Gathering up enough energy once more, she opens her mouth to its widest to scream. Nothing comes out. At least, nothing she can hear.

Her breasts pop out, full and firm.

This cannot be happening! He can't! He's my father! He'll stop! He has to! Her panic is racing and hot.

She uses an arm to shield her agitated breasts with desperate haste. She can scream loudly enough for someone to hear. She knows she can. And she tries, but again she chokes. She smites him. He takes it without flinching, grinning instead, jeeringly. She feels his cold, thick fingers dig into her hip curves, prying at the lacy waistband of her panties. An upsurge of disgust combined with survival and strength wells up within her. She tries to hold off his brawny, sweaty arms with her other hand, but her palm and fingers are too small to close around his, and he is both too slippery and too strong. He has animal strength.

No. She will fight. Her breasts could be exposed now, but she doesn't care. She will. So she does. She uses whatever she has left in her to beat her balled fists against his chest and face, struggling with all the might of the desperate, protecting what can be taken but never recovered. He's struggling with all his might too, not because he has to but because the melodrama of his actions somewhat taunts her. He grunts and howls, trying to satiate the want for her that has gnawed at him since she was thirteen, trying to satiate the foul thoughts of her that have haunted him since he began feeding his lust by spying on her when she bathed, as the shower sprinkled, as the water cascaded on and pushed the soap suds off the curves of her round hips and the swell of her breasts until she shone. He lets out little roars of pleasure, 'struggling' with her.

"Daddy, please," she whispers through her tears, finally realizing the futility of her physical strength and the strength that might yet be stored up in her words. "Daddy, please. Don't … don't do …" She struggles a little as he asserts a thumb and a forefinger over hers. "… do not do … do not do this …" The remainder of the words get hiccupped away.

Her pleas do not merit a reply.

There are no sounds now except her blood-choked whimpers and his abrupt breath, obscenely timed to match hers. His lips shut over her nipple, and he sucks hungrily, squeezing the other and crushing it between his fingers.

She squirms, pleading again in a voice gone shaky as she looks up at him, her mind willing strength to her arms. "Papa … please …"

His belt clinks as he frees it from the loops of his trousers. He falls on her with as much control as one deboned would.

She looks for God in those moments, but God is hidden. She thrashes with ebbing strength; pushes against his chest, claws savagely at his back, feeling the strips of skin roll beneath her broken nails in five slippery strips. He howls with pain that seems to fuel his masochistic desire. Strength detonates in him. He grabs her hands and tosses them far apart; they hit the ground with such force that they lay sprawled and without strength. He rips her panties apart with a single snap—a sound she'll remember as 'long' as she lives—and eases his trousers off, one leg after the other.

"Papa ... pl ... ea ... se."

He pries open those thighs, heaves down with all his might, feels for and breaks through her in one rough, frictional thrust, having no desire to be gentle. She jerks backward and shuts her eyes tightly in pain that plunges through her like a spear's stab. (But pain? No, not even that. Anguish. Pure anguish.) He thrusts harder. A scream gets caught in her throat. He submerges himself farther into her. A banana lobe passing through the eye of a needle.

With each movement of his body, with each grunt of pleasure, she sees in her mind's eye the seams of all her carefully stitched wishes snapping loose, the foundations of her meticulously built dreams crumbling, shattering into a thousand pieces. She will never have the joy and satisfaction of seeing her husband smiling down at her proudly. She will never have kids. She will never have a family. No, not with this injustice done to her.

His groans distracts her thoughts as he shudders against her, struggling to go deeper and deeper, his savage desire to explore walls untouched flaring. Pure anguish like a wet whiplash wipes at her in relentless strokes.

Slowly, her eyes open. Through the wet, sticky fringes of her lashes, she stares beyond him at the ceiling, her vacant eyes bright with unshed tears. She hears his open mouth twitching. It seems to open wider with each thrust. She sees the trickles of sweat on his forehead, running down the strong veins of his face. She sees the lazy roll of his eyes that reflects the peak of his ecstasy. He's looking down at her and smiling, the filth and infamy in him exposed like nakedness. She sees how much he likes this. How would anyone like this?

Her nostrils flare and her lips tighten as spasms of nausea sweep through her. She feels a zillion pinpricks explode at the back of her eyes. Tears spill around the bruise on her temple. He eases his tempo. His agitated breath fans her face, but her nostrils are too blocked with phlegm to perceive it. He goes much faster now, savoring the helplessness of his prey. It hurts, but she doesn't make any sound. She doesn't have it in her to scream curses. There's no reason to do that, for she knows she won't be alive much longer to see him suffer through the special kind of hell she knows has already been prepared for him. There's no—

He stops abruptly and arches his back, the expression on his face making him more animal than is possibly conceivable. He makes a thin, long moan of ecstasy, jerkig like one convulsing through the prick. Again. And again. And again. She feels him strongly inside her as he squirts into her belly. He stops moving for some seconds. Probably three. She feels him go slowly limp and slide out of the bruised, swollen, crimson flesh of her vagina. She feels the syrupy coolness from his prick drop onto and drip down her burning thigh, flowing down to meet the map of darkened blood beneath her on the floor. He sighs in content, rises unhurriedly and a little unsteadily to his feet, flings his trousers and shirt over his shoulder, and walks away in unruffled, impenitent calm, naked, staggering, and humming.

The mirror is still there, its surface a still, inaudible testament to the happenings of that day. The sun is still shining, its hard brilliance slashing through the flimsy curtains and making a golden-silvery puddle just beside her. The air has suddenly become stale and suffocating. She's alone, struggling to breathe normally, her eyes clouded and stinging with hurt, her hair scattered over her face in unruly waves. She's lying on the irreparable tatters of a once-beautiful dress, staring through tears springing from the depths of her soul at the reflection of a once-beautiful girl, clamped in the thoughts of the unfairness of what has just been done her, and feeling reduced to a revolting object of pity. There's nothing in her. It's one thing to lose something. It's another to be aware you've lost it. She's not of the dignity she thought someone of dignity might have taken, lacking the pride that was uniquely hers. And yes, she knows she is not. She can feel the bits and pieces of the little she has left scattered inside her.

Her father, the one who gave her life and helped give birth to her, has inflicted indignity on her and has done so with brazen savagery and cruel disregard. There's nothing left of the dress she had loved that morning. There's nothing left of the frail innocence she'd had that morning. There's nothing left of her, or for her either. Maybe the memories of Ma. Maybe a noose swinging from the fan. Or, just maybe, a short note written in the barest of words, spattered with teardrops, held in place by an empty bottle of sleeping pills, the contents which have been slowly swallowed.

The Yo-Yo and The Harlot

You know how houses overlooking busy streets are at night. You get drawn by the hubbub down below, and you might sit by the window. Things catch your attention, some strange, like the octogenarian with the clay-clad feet, judged, convicted, and sentenced insane by poverty, laboriously pushing a barrowful of crappy scrap, leaving you wondering if at some earlier point in his life he had seen himself in someone else and had said, "God forbid." Or you might see a huddle of dowdily dressed men around a stand, giving more news than the newspaper, deciphering words and interspersing imagined meanings, interchanging and interconnecting cloudy perceptions, frowning, formulating dubious theories, supplementing the half known, ballooning it into an acceptance of a unanimously endorsed "known," which, invariably, turns to a whole 'nother topic of hot debate of hellbent head banging, powerful palm pounding, finger flinging, and spittle swapping. You might see a mother chasing her girl child, catching up with her, yanking her off the ground by the ear whilst viciously spanking till her cries grow so high-pitched the sound disappears altogether. You might see several hundred school children storming down the road like a desert army of conquered strays.

So there I sat in my window, observing these things, sometimes appalled, a few times indifferent or nostalgic, sometimes shocked, other times curious, like when I saw this particular young fellow I'm about to tell a story about.

I had taken no interest in him, had not even seen him till, well, till he decided to cross the road with headphones stuck in and nearly got knocked eight feet through the air. And even when the driver's horn kept honking, even when the near manslaughterer had stuck out his head with his palms splayed, swearing with a loud voice, decreeing curses on the bastards's father and his father before him, the "idiot" kept on walking, bobbing his head, break-dancing his shoulders, and tapping and swiping his screen. He had escaped death without even knowing it.

"A yo-yo," I whispered to myself and chuckled, sneering at him and his yo-yo ways.

He glanced left and right, apparently unsure where to go. Not unsure because he had mixed paths but because this was something of a wander. So he looked to both sides again, made to go to the right, decided on the left, walked a few paces in, and finally decided to be decisive enough to reverse, go left, and keep going left.

Confused yo-yo, I thought, subsequently picking up an interest in him as soon as he cut into a street corner, walking down that lane I knew so well. If it had been a little interesting prior to this point, now the tempo had begun to throb, but slowly. I rose from where I sat and then mounted a stool for better view.

She was coming from the opposite end, dark with smoothness sleek as oil-paint black, wearing a top that stopped short of the navel and a pair of loose shorts that stopped at the tops of her thighs, the part that starts to look like baseball. She was walking leisurely, her hips pendulums.

He, the yo-yo boy whose eyes had been on his phone, he who very nearly would've been smashed to smatters, he with an unbalanced mind and indecisiveness so severe, it was he who, at this point, decided to break whatever focus he had with what was so intent on killing him, lifted his eyes, and saw her. I could tell their eyes met, for their movements slowed with the mutual mental sizing up—faint wariness on the yo-yo's part, in stark comparison to the crude and brazen invitation on the girl's. Proximity lessened between them till there was no more than a gap the length of his full erection.

It was like in the movies. This dramatic meeting. It was like in the movies. This tightened silence between them housing a mixture of wonder, of fear and seduction. The way she tenderly encircled his neck with her arms, bunched herself to him like a cold, lonely ball, raised herself on her toes, and kissed him right there, damning public decorum. He stiffened in shock, observed his surroundings as much as he could with his lips still locked to hers, yielded helplessly, let himself loose, and turned up wild. But it was at that point, when his pleasure had shot as sharply upward as the clean, clear sound of a finger snap, that she let go. He ogled her, dazed. He wanted more. Would do anything for the bottom of the icing he had licked off her tongue, off her lips. Would do anything to devour the cake beneath that the sexy stranger had offered sans his asking.

I watched, a little horrified, and my curiosity rose, as must have the hard-on of the speci-man I was watching.

Her hands were moving. At that moment, I wanted nothing more than to hear whatever she was saying, but to risk moving from where I was, running all the way down and being that nosy, would mean me forfeiting the unfolding scenes of this play that promised to be one of intrigue, suspense, and romance. So I stayed where I was, interpreting her gestures as best I could (his too), the sly gesturing of her slender arm, the direction at the end of it, the demure cock of her head, her shoulders bunching from cold, his head vigorously nodding and then thrown back in the kind of exaggerated laughter that precedes sudden promised pleasure.

And then they walked.

"Like an ox to the slaughter," I sneered because I was jealous and mad and envious that such "sudden promised pleasure" had never met me, who had always been here. "Like a fool to the correction of the stocks," I spat.

But he hesitated. She slowly shook her head. He stretched on tiptoe, cocking his head this way and that in the direction she had pointed. "Didn't she have a man?" he seemed to be asking. "Wasn't he at home?" Her ass cheeks seemed to spread as she walked, as she ignored his question and locked his hands in hers, leading the way, planting them on that ass. The house, hers, was close by, just to the left. I would see the end of this play, I vowed as I ran to my kitchen to scramble onto my cabinet, where I could get a slight view of what I hoped was her room, the scene of sex.

So they fell into the room, its walls caved and its texture rendered soft by the glow the lamp flames' yellow threw on it. She turned at once and planted kiss seedlings on his neck, his chest, up to his lips, his ears, as she unbuttoned his shirt, as she dragged him to the bed behind her. He unwound his arms from that damned shirt straitjacketing his passion. I couldn't see more, for they had dropped below eye level. Just his thin behind flying up and going down in what I knew to be a brutal series of thrusts. I felt me rise. But then, just as I tipped higher—or tried to—I caught a movement behind him, then a figure emerging from the shadows, solidifying. My erection shrunk instantly.

A man. A huge man. A huge man with a knife curved as a horn, twisted as death, the edge serrated as a shark's, so serrated that each tooth, small as they were, made striking outlines against those thrown glows.

What was happening? I had become frantic, confused, terrified, horrified.

And then my question was answered. As the yo-yo's thin behind flew up, his head rising and his mouth slowly widening in tiding pleasure, the man's hand lunged forward with such force, the flight of which motion couldn't capture. I cringed in terror as the murderous hand shook and twisted, detached high up in the air, and plunged in again. And again. And again. Seconds passed. It seemed to me as a dream might. Who had he stabbed? The yo-yo? The harlot? The yo-yo and the harlot?

Time as long as a year passed, me transfixed, slowly feeling my mind shedding.

Then the girl, with the motion of one rising from a slippery bath, stood and wiped herself, between her thighs first and then her hands, her torso, and her face, looking back at what I imagined to be the struggling, blood-slobbering near-carcass of the yo-yo.

"Like an ox to the slaughter," I repeated as I flipped from the page of Proverbs chapter 7, as I penned the last words of this tale as told by it, as I saw in my mind's eye the harlot and her man hurriedly flee from the scene of a crime only broda Solo and this writer knows.

Man Whore War

O n one of those days when there was nothing to wake up early for, we headed for Enugu Street, me and Omoba the Silent. We waved down a keke and got into it, ignoring the rider's greetings, his enquiries for direction, and his overall presence. Omoba would point out the directions with a "here," a "there," and an "enter there." A series of heres and theres later had us standing in front of a beat-up, rundown building. Neon lights (already broken) surrounded the letters that made up its name, Bristol. A handful of men littering its passage cuddled beers and puffed ciggies, sleep and drink (or high) controlling their movements. The smell about them was so oppressively pungent, it seemed to have a personality of its own, one we carefully wove around, careful not to initiate the slightest of contact for fear of having it reach out and cling to us like it had them. We were inside in seconds.

Now this was quite a place, this Bristol. Some DJ was screeching here, a bevy of whores gossiping there, mics hanging and speakers blaring somewhere, a combination of equipment too scanty for a space so big. The sheer amount of smoke softened the disco lights to a glow, blurring the people that leaned against the railings to silent little ghosts that swam.

As we searched for somewhere to be, I glanced at Omoba. He was scrunching his nose (like I had done since the moment we arrived). We passed people half seated, half lying in their seats with a crateful of bottles, a heap of ciggy butts, and a TV that noiselessly flashed images in their midst. We located a table in a far corner with two empty seats, wiped the dust and dried beer off of them, and ordered a Guinness, a big-ass stout, and a plateful of big-ass snails. Then we sat sipping, crunching, and observing for a half hour, commenting on this horrid little place of sin we didn't see ourselves leaving in a hurry. A smiling, crimson-faced whore with breasts (I thought were) rolled all the way to the top approached us.

"Una no go fuck?" she asked, leaning over, staring directly at Omoba like he owed her feelings and a fuck.

He stared at her, took a thoughtful sip, and pinned a piece of snail with his toothpick. "Jago," he said after swallowing. "I dey come." And then he left, chewing as they went, his hand in hers.

I am of the shy breed, see? I'd die before doing things if there were a chance I'd be watched or even noticed, because my movements start to change and heat rushes up my neck and reddens my face and I feel like everyone is drawing curious bows with eyes for arrows that shoot into my back and my too-big-a-butt-for-a-boy. But I'd been here a while. The plate lay empty, and the beer was in my bladder, and my bladder was boiling because I'd held it in for like, an hour. Boy, I had to pee. It would have been better if Omoba were here, as he'd have accompanied me and made my shame and shyness less noticeable.

So where in Bristol was Omoba? He hadn't returned, and it seemed strange. Who spent an hour kpanshing a whore? Omoba did. If he could spend a half hour shining his shoes before rush-hour classes (when others spent seconds or none), I reasoned he could go as far as requesting an STD test from a whore before whoring. Na dah kain man e be. He never rushed anything, and if you made him, he only took more time. But, ha! An hour whoring whores who are, as I'd heard from veteran whore-whorers, infamous for their briskness with time and brusqueness in manners? It sure seemed strange, funny even. My cock veins stung. Without thinking, I stood up and headed to the bar.

"How far?" I yelled to the barman. "You know where to piss dey?"

He jerked up a thumb. "Upstair."

"Upstairs?"

"Yes. E dey corner."

I left and ascended the stairs past one or two advanced men in agbada hurriedly descending with their heads hanging; past a boy with jaunty steps and a toothpick in his mouth, fastening his belt; past a whore who I would later know as Nice casually telling the other whore, "I wan fuck dis boy," and then me, "I wan fuck you for free." Of course, I smiled and said no even when that piece of barely clad ass reached for my eyeballs and popped it. I walked past rooms with ladies in fishnets, gossiping, and a bored one in a flimsy gown who had a temper that made her snap "Ashawo!" at me. Some at the doors slowly stepped from foot to foot, tracing their middle fingers from their necks down their already parted gowns, revealing bare breasts or saggy breasts or bleached breasts or stretch-marked breasts or tired breasts, a few firm breasts, some pear-shaped, some pea-sized.

"You wan fuck?" one asked, suddenly reaching out to drag me into her den.

I felt the lust in me stir and whirl, and yes, I so much wanted to fuck, to press my face right up her ass as I held her hips in place, but this brazenness alarmed the fuck out of me, and I simpered and scampered.

"Please, you know where the toilet dey?" I asked one washing clothes, my eyes down. She pointed "there," and her wrappa fell off her shoulders, revealing a pair of breasts that swung slow and heavy. "There" was a latrine with tissues, shit, pads, and hair risen right up to the surface. I pissed in it with a closed-eyed grimace, trying to drown out the smell, the sight, and the sound that piss makes upon hard surface. No, I could never have sex around here, I vowed to my pride. These hoes had squatted to shit here, several hundreds of them. Lawd only knew the spate of diseases they'd contacted and exchanged! But I knew I was all but trying to convince myself, for when I got out and saw Nice once again clapping her hands as she chatted with a friend, her perversely slender waist undulating under that miniskirt split all the way up to the crack of her ass, I knew I was in trouble, and that same lawd I swore to knew I really couldn't care less.

Nice's room was gloomy. The ceilings were low, the bulb glowed drab and green, a sorry little cupboard leaned against a corner, and three netted beds that had no business being there, one on either side and a third at the head of both, made every available passage cramped, the proximity between us the length of a finger, and the fragrance of her perfume strangling. She turned, sat on the third bed, and smiled at me, patting beside her.

"So how you dey na?" she whispered, her face in my neck and her palms spread over my fly, rubbing, gathering what erection there was in her fingers. "See how your skin fresh! Ah! See how e fair!"

I chuckled uneasily, maybe shyly. My mind was racing, thinking exactly what I was getting myself into. I'd heard tales of spirits and demons inhabiting these ones, transferring themselves like spirits into swine.

She must have noticed my tenseness, for she continued, "I tink I tell you say I go fuck you for free? You no wan gree, abi?"

I'd heard stories of graceless, luckless folks contacting HIV and herpes from their firsts. I didn't want to fuck anymore, but I didn't have the courage to say so because she'd already slipped off her skirt and, with no panties on, oh my lawdee, the sheen of light plastering those thighs made them smoother and rounder. I reached for them, attempting to bury my breath between, but I sensed resistance and looked up to see a smile that wasn't there come on immediately when my eyes met hers. "Stop na! I no be your babe joor!"

"But I fit be your guy na?" I managed to say, still fondling, finding myself falling in love with a whore.

"You bring life jacket?" she asked, ignoring my question, sidestepping my touch, rising on her knees to the cupboard.

"Wetin be—?"

"Off your trouser na! Na your first time to fuck ashawo be dis?"

I was still there, hearing the echo of the spite in her tone, when she unbuttoned my trousers, knelt, pulled them down to midthigh, stroked my prick, and before doing the lil' suck thingy, told me "Na three-five for short time!"

"No wahala!"

She wore me the "life jacket," said I had "small dick o!" and, before she lay down to spread her legs apart, said, "But you for pay me first oo!"

"I go pay you na. I wan run?"

Her face twitched as I lay over her for a kiss.

"You for pay me first oo," she whispered, trying to smile. "You know say some kain men, dey no dey like pay." She added, when I thought she had stopped. "Jus pay na."

I thought I should shut her up, that paying would be the noble thing. I felt for my back pocket, counted a couple of thousands and handed it to her. That was all I had. That was silly for that is when— as soon as she counted the money and hid it from sight—I saw the real whore in her rear horn. It began to happen really fast.

"Abeg, do fast," she snapped, scooping pomade with her middle finger to moisten her pussy. "Your time begins now." A judge couldn't have sounded sterner.

I could feel my enthusiasm drain off as loudly as the end of a straw at the bottom of a bottle. But still, I knew I had to fuck her, to pound her, to cum and get my money's worth. I tried to be tender with her, to simper like a loyal lover, to kiss her, to let her know she was being loved by me, that I didn't see her as the whore as others did. So I reached for a kiss.

"Abeg abeg abeg, carry your beer face commot my mouth abeg."

I shut my eyes as tight as I could trying to concentrate and summon an erection, but it wouldn't work, so I decided to try rolling off the shirt shielding her breasts so I could suck, but, "I no be your babe, abeg," she kept snapping, getting increasingly irritated at my presence and agitated. "Your time dey go o, make I just tell you now!" And she followed that with a long hiss.

I slipped my flaccid cock in, and in there was the most juiceless, most unwelcome piece of pussy I'd been in all my life. The strokes started, first slow and tender, then faster and stronger as I held up a leg onto my shoulder, clutched an ass cheek apart for easier access, and tried to focus my mind's eye on the best piece of pussy I'd been in. I went in as hard as I could, pounding through to the hilt, but each time I surreptitiously opened an eye to spy on her expression, her lips were pursed, her brows were arched, and the "ahhs" and "oohs" and moans I found pretentious and therefore ego-flattening came out with little passive-aggressive hisses in between.

"You no sabi fuck sef?" she taunted with spite and, this time, an aggressive hiss. Jesus fucking Christ! Wasn't I a customer? Wasn't she supposed to make me feel good?

I shut my eyes so tightly I could feel the whole of my body quiver and focused my mind more specifically on that sexyass girl I summoned in my mind's eye each time I wanked, willing the whole of me to cum. Yes, it had begun to come. I could feel it. I heard her voice in the di`````stance as I increased the stride of my strokes.

"Abeg o, no break my toto bone because of 3K o!" Hiss. She was moaning now, but I knew it was as fake as the smile that had lured me into this.

"Aaaah, aaaaaah, ooooooh!"

I came but it felt nothing like that. Felt more like, and as ordinary as, spittle leaving mouth. She eased herself from under me in a way that felt like a push, pulled the condom off of me so spitefully it snapped and flung cum, wiped my cock with a tissue as she did, and whispered more to me than to herself, "Mtcheeew. All these men wey no sabi fuck sef." She left me lying there, silently cursing Omoba, viciously hating myself, and feeling like one of the shits I had just pissed on.

A Place Between
Sky and Earth

Today it is deep and solemn on Facebook. Pricked by curiosity, I tap off free data mode and scroll through; pictures materialize and the horrors they represent unfold: a raging ball of yellow suspended in sky-blotting black smoke, a queue of cars caught up in flames right at its bottom, the varying captions in caps lock underneath communicating urgency. It happened a few moments back … and it is still happening.

I am struck numb.

From the tidbits of information and snatches of reports I catch as I scroll through the graphic photos of stretched bodies roasted stiff, I gather that this happened in Berger; that a tanker had lost control of its brakes; that the tanker's driver had attempted to regain control but tipped his tank instead and crashed; that a spark had spat a flame; and that the explosion had set off a blood-chilling chain reaction. Vehicles had swiftly caught fire, dozens of people, pumped by panic, had struggled to flee all at once, the greater number were unsuccessful, the victims lit up, bodies blazing and wriggling and screaming and thrashing. Bodies dropping. Forty cars and their occupants burned to death, I've gathered. Sixty-something, some insist. There's a video, which I click and view. The inferno, even from a distance, fills the screen, the blackness of its smoke horrifying. Explosions boom every handful of seconds for the next few minutes. Cars, together with the people in them. The recorder is a woman. Her voice is shaky. She is stuttering. "See people ooo!" she cries. "See cars, oh my God!" The video swivels. There are no firefighters in sight. Just people with cameras gathered in clusters.

But it is not macabre humor that locks me to the disaster raging on the other side of my screen. It is a premonition with hackles raised. It is dread curled like a ready viper in the pit of my stomach, striking now, striking hard. It is goosebumps popping up over my arms and thighs. I slump backward and then pick myself up a minute later, slip my phone into my pocket, and venture out to get a drink from The Bar Ten Streets Away. I will not face whatever this is until I'm there. So at that table, in that hidden bar, on that hidden street where people give as much fucks to pilferers as they do to pastors, I signal a guy with a wink to bring a smoke and a drink. I drain the chilled contents of Alomo Bitters within the hour. Then I take a casual walk to the back, where there's a bunch of skimpily dressed whores kissing blunts. I overhear one ask the other if she's heard about "d faya."

"D faya? Which faya?" the other asks. Her voice is distant and disinterested.

The teller seems genuinely surprised. "You sure say you dey Naija?" She whips out her phone, smacking the smoke clouds over her face and bending low to show.

I take long drags, clapping out thick clouds. The blunt smothers in the wind and gets reduced to a glowing stub that I flick away. I dust off my hands and calmly dial Vandra. I know that silence on the line, the one that precedes numbers that are either unreachable or switched off. The silence stretches; the network bars deplete;

the reception flounders. My breath is held unconsciously. Then the operator's voice: "The number you're trying to call is currently switched off. Please try again later. Thank you."

I feel my bowels fill up. I suddenly want to shit. I try her number one more time. Same thing, same voice. I try not to think of anything negative as I walk home. Because Vandra works just outside of Berger.

It is nearing evening, and Tiger gens are starting to convulse. They cough smoke from every corner. Vandra hasn't returned. By now, talk about the disaster is rife. It is all over the telly; it is blaring over the radio. I can hear the neighbors talking about it and wailing in loud voices, describing the gory contents of their imaginations, of trapped people, of mingled screams and hands that tried to shield them, of bodies that had the breath sucked out of them. I am in my house, silent, my guts knotting and biting as I dial Vandra. I try to convince myself that she never passed Berger today, or that in the event that she did, she had done so long before or after that tanker tipped over. The operator says the same thing into my ear. No. I refuse to accept that. There are people who can't just die, people whose lives steer past and weave about the shadows mishaps cast. Vandra is one of them. The thought comforts me. But as evening thickens, the knots tighten. I try to imagine life without Vandra, but the thought is too impossible, too much to bear.

I am in a vacuum. Cold sweat is starting to sheath me.

My cell starts to ring. It's funny the way our minds make connections, how in those short milliseconds before my eyes swivel to the screen I conclude that it is Vandra calling and start to praise the Lord. But I snatch it up, and my heart sinks. It is Lala.

There's a tremendous rumble of noise around her, but she yells above it. "Did you hear about the fire?"

"Yes," I say.

"It is terrible. The pictures! And that is exactly where Vandra passes."

The knots have started to grow teeth. They sink them into my sides at the mention of her name.

"May God help this country—"

I say yes to the prayer as confidently as I can in the exact moment that Lala asks if Vandra is home yet. I stutter, trying to tell her I meant yes to another thing, that Vandra isn't home yet, but not before she says in a rush, "Oh, she's home? Thank you, Jesus! I'll soon be home too. Love you." She hangs up.

Okay. So Lala will come within the hour, and when she does, how do I begin to tell her that our girl isn't home? I dial Vandra, and the operator comes on pretty fast, like she's pretty pissed at my determined insistence. She says the "*NUMBER*" I'm trying to call is "*SWITCHED OFF!*" If I could ask her, at least, if she could help locate where exactly the phone was turned off, wouldn't I have?

The thought of Vandra burning in a bus or trapped in some cab, her clothes swiftly eaten off her skin, repulses me into prayers and divine declarations—"God, you *cannot lie*. God, you *will* spare your *own*. God you have *spared* her"—even though part of my mind tells me that if she was there, she was there, and if she wasn't, she wasn't. "I cover her with the blood of Jesus," I repeat till I think I feel peace settle upon my spirit. I know Vandra is coming. I know her phone's battery is drained or something. I know she's taking a little longer doing what she's doing. I take two and then three shots of some drink and feel my chest explode, giving off sparks that I interpret as hope; I feel more hopeful than I've been.

Then I hear Lala's car some forty minutes later and begin to feel my spirit tremble. And crumble.

Lala has soft brown eyes. Now these eyes widen, registering the faintest amusement. She's searching my face for hints of the joke she's hesitating to fully respond to, but she can't find any.

"I don't think I understand what you're saying," she says, lowering herself to an armrest. "Where is Vandra? You told me Vandra was home just under an hour ago. Now you're saying Vandra has not come?"

I feel my heartbeat accelerate as I slowly walk to her. I don't know how I can handle what I feel for both of us now, but whatever happens, happens. I watch her dial someone—Vandra, most definitely. She holds the phone to her ear, and she's whispering something earnestly, snapping her fingers. She rises from the armrest and moves into the corridor. I follow her in.

"They are saying the number is switched off," she says as she turns to me, the beauty-ruining misery of her expression shattering me, making me earnestly ask God to just spare us Vandra, to not let the glimpse of what Lala has just shown balloon into a portrait.

I place my hands on her shoulders, and that is when I see them shake. I rock her as gently as I can. In a voice trying to feed calm, I whisper, "Listen, Lala. You have to be calm about this. This is just news. Vandra is fine. I know it … and God knows it."

She regards me with uncertainty, and again those sad eyes crush my heart and the smile I've worn.

"Let's go to the sitting room."

It is in times of storm that certain love toughens. She and I—she'll be sixty-four next month—we shuffle through the dark, narrow passage to the sitting room, where I sit her down, squat before her, and make her breathe. "Breathe, Mami. Breathe. Smile. Hmm?"

I try to initiate a smile, but the weight of what I feel inside makes my face feel too much like the bark of an oak to do shit.

She blinks, trying to smile back, and for the first time in decades, I notice the wrinkles around her eyes, the elderly, enduring version we'd said our hearts would grow to be.

Then, crying, she says, "What would happen to us, to me, if something happened to her? Her number is not even going now. Maybe the fire has burned everything, melted everything—"

"Mami," I cut in, sounding stern but feeling fake, "stop saying that. What are you doing? Don't you know you are killing her with your own words already?" I reach out to her, and she bites her lips as if to bite back the words, but she's really biting them because there's pain in each of us that we might wish for others not to see but that will be too great for them not to see. It makes those lips quiver, and she crumbles to me. I hold her tightly, and she sobs while I silently ask God why it has to be us. The evening wears deeper, sloughing into night. None of the neighbors know what is happening in the little apartment of the pastor and his wife. I prefer to keep it so with just Lala by my side and the God (that called me) hearing us.

The bulbs and tellies from the neighbors' houses throw light into our dark, silent space. Nine ticks to ten, then ten to eleven, but Vandra isn't back and neither is her number available. We call the only friend we know she has, a guy called Didier. The first thing Didier does (when we introduce ourselves as Vandra's parents) is ask if we've heard from Vandra and if we heard about the fire. About Vandra, we say no as our hearts sink, and about the fire, I say yes but tell him to relax, that Vandra will soon be coming home.

It's past eleven.

Twelve meets Lala in heart-wrenching tears and desperate, whispered pleas to God. Twelve meets my heart thrown down, kicked, and trampled. This night is silent. Lala is made frail by cold as she looks out the window. I am right by her. When God says joy comes in the morning, does he include his prophets, his pastors?

There is no morning the next morning. Just a continuation of what would (or could) be a life of nights and darker nights. I have scrolled through Facebook. I have seen the pictures with images of mayhem from different angles, from closer and clearer proximities. I have seen the bodies hanging from the windows, trapped and killed in escape. I have seen those trapped in that bus with the yellow paint peeled off. I have seen the queue of burnt corpses held in death in different rigid, twisted, bent, wilted, naked positions. I have looked for anyone resembling a girl. A lithe girl of sixteen. I have zoomed closer and tried to discern features with my eyes clouded and blinded with the stifled tears of the numbed and the stunned.

When Lala thinks I am not looking, I see her looking closely at the pictures on her Facebook screen, like she is trying (like me when she wasn't looking) to identify Vandra. Here it is, morning, and here I am, hoping, crying, challenging God to work out something Four Hebrew Boys style, cursing at heaven's silence, and trying to let Lala not hear. Here it is, morning, and here I am, my mind a freeform sketch of imaginations, pleasant and gory: Vandra burning; Vandra in heaven; Vandra somewhere safe, free and alive, ignorant that she's being worried off her parents' minds; Vandra desperately trying to reach me. That thought starts to work out a smile on my face, one that wilts when Lala walks in.

"They are packing the … bodies in bags," she says, staring at me. Her eyes are sunken already. Her eyeballs have red threaded veins in them. "Why us?" I hear her whisper. "Why us?"

I look down and nod simply because when there's no strength in you, nodding is all you can manage. I tell her to stop, but I can't face her now. Neither will I be able to anytime soon in years to come. "We'll go and identify…her," I say.

Immediately when I say that, I feel my comportment quiver and dissolve like webs above a flame. I am suddenly stunned by life and the reward God has chosen, in all his wisdom, to award me. Grief wants to cut through my knees and break me down, but I refuse, clenching my teeth much like my fists. This isn't the sentence I hoped Vandra would be in any day of our lives. Now I was talking about identifying her charred body? My girl getting burned while the fucking creator I'm serving watches, letting (or even making) it happen? I judder till I keep still, Lala's arms my buffer until hope resurfaces and fights itself afloat. Vandra is alive.

"Let's go and check anyway to clear any doubts, but I know God is on the throne and she is not in any of them." We agree.

Since this started, we have awkwardly stopped using Vandra's name in the same or any sentence that would land some credibility to the violation of our self-professed faith. I head to the bathroom and splash water over my face and hair. I meet Lala in the sitting room. She is made smaller and subdued, sober, by the scarf wound round and round her head like a small potato. She runs her palms over the stubble on my chin, taps, and tells me I haven't shaved well, but I tell her I am keeping my lucky beard for us, and she manages a smile. We shut our eyes and say a little prayer. We thank God that he has protected "his daughter" and give him an ultimatum based on the promises of verse 118 of chapter 32 that Vandra be back. Then we step out.

The air is dry and fresh and somehow looks the color of silver. This morning is too crisp for such things; the death that precedes our steps and our thoughts, that haunts our smiles and our faith. The baker is brushing his teeth and trying to smuggle words out the corner of his mouth to engage fully in the typical early morning small compound gossip. He and the rest of the cluster raise their hands in salute, half bowing to greet Lala and me.

"Daddy!"

"Good morning, Pastor!"

"Good morning," we reply. "How are you?" I say.

"Fine, Daddy," they echo.

"How's our beautiful girl?" one of them asks.

I feel Lala's fingers tighten around mine. An involuntary gesture, I know. I don't know what to do, but I'm already at it. I smile and say she's fine before we, Lala and me, turn to go to the morgue.

A signboard with a faded arrow in it directs us with the last of its shine to the first morgue, which is, from the info we've gathered, a bungalow at the end of a street filled with potholes full with water. Our keke napep weaves through shriveled slivers of tarred road, bounces into badly negotiated routes, and seems to heightens the tension that Lala and I have in us. Two more bends and we ride into a slightly rowdy crowd in front of the bungalow, folks of faint hopes and fearsome faith. My heart chooses to think anything as Lala and I alight the taxi. We pay the driver and walk in with all the humility of the hopeful, joining the crowd.

I ask the first most sober-looking young man I see if he's … he's, you know, searching for someone he *might* have "lost." He says "sure," trying to look strong. He's pretty frank about it, that he's searching for his twin brother, that the proprietor hasn't come yet and the mortuaries cannot be opened without his say-so. Lala is by me, listening to the young man talk. Something has turned her inside out and she has started to cry. I tell the young man to excuse me, and he apologizes like he caused it and walks away.

"She is not here," I whisper to Lala as I hold her, hug her, and take her aside. "You hear me, Mami? She is not here."

"How would you know that?" she says out of the broken whispers of questioned hopes that have now become her heart.

"*I know.* We prayed this morning, and we are in a covenant with God. Don't you know you're in a covenant with God? We're his sons and daughters, and nothing bad is happening to his children who are in a covenant with him."

"But God, why us?" she says.

It hurts that she's heard nothing I've just said.

"The proprietor of the place is coming soon," I tell her. "Get yourself together. Let's go and look for somewhere to sit. Oya, Smile!"

So we go somewhere to sit on a wall, silently sing praises to God (somewhat tentatively), and tell him to take control. We are not the only ones doing this; others are openly praying. Somewhere away from all this, a little boy wearing the wrong flip-flop on each foot is sitting close to someone who looks like his father; both are silent, in their own worlds, with their own stories, without someone who is supposed to be in it.

The proprietor, surprisingly early for a person who is needed, comes some twenty minutes later, a chewing stick jutting from between his lips, bobbing. The rowdiness of the crowd quickly mellows to a low hum. The proprietor exudes no grace. His gracelessness is made manifest in the gruff, strictly master-servant manner he uses to speak to the employees and the people. After a few minutes, we see the mortuary attendants disperse, disinfect themselves, and get ready to open the various doors. The still in the crowd is chilled at the fringes. We fall into a queue that stretches from the dark unseen in the bungalow to a few yards before the gate. Then we fill out perfunctory forms before collecting tickets, each with a serial number. The serial numbers are grouped into contained batches, and together each batch's "members" go looking for their missing or suspected dead. Thirty-seven people have been brought here since yesterday, the "receptionist" tells us with sympathy that has lost its taste from repetition.

"Dia are a lot of women in one room, some girls, some boys, very few men. Diaris a room—the attendant there will show you—for those looking for small, small children. Diawaz a school bus with some nursery school people in it. Those people have their own separate rooms for easy arrangement." He pauses and summons warmth to his eyes and lips. "But I know God will not allow any of your own to be there. In Jesus's name."

The crowd shouts a loud amen, and I am unsettled. There is something wrong with all this that I can't quite pinpoint. I wonder whose will be there and what God might have to say about that.

I hold Lala throughout our wait, and we talk about food, the weather, what we'll do when we see Vandra, how we will spin and spank her when we return home to see her squatting at the door, and … and if it was wise for Lala to go with me to 'sift' through the bodies.

"Don't use 'identify,'" Lala cautions me half-seriously, half-playfully. "We don't have anybody to 'identify' there."

I smile in deference. "Okay, Mami."

"But I still want to see."

"Don't vomit."

"Am I kissing them?"

A quick, sudden giggle spurts out of my mouth and then hers. It's so strange that in this place where everyone is hefting rucksacks of distant hopes through this cold charged clime of suspense, of death, that two people are openly sharing laughter. At what joke? One or two disgusted glares settle on us, and I instantly fall into the somber moment, but Lala smiles first before she falls. It melts me, that smile, but not for the reason you think. Listen. What I want most in this world now is for my cell to ring, for Vandra to be at the other end of the line, for me to suppress my excitement swiftly enough to not give a clue as I pass the phone to Lala, for me to find and watch the other side of this struggling glow of a smile she's wearing, the one that widens in pure bliss and causes broken brackets about our eyes.

Our batch is called in the midst of my daydream. We all stand and crawl like hesitant turtles from our various corners to where attendants gesture and usher us into the gender-specific rooms. I feel Lala's hand slip into mine, and I squeeze it till the warmth of mine generates into hers. We filter into the room for female remains, and the heavily preserved, vague-smelling unnatural cool smacks us straight in the lungs. Silence. Someone directly behind me shrieks softly, probably seeing the body I'm staring at and am strangely hooked to now. It is the shape and size of a teenager, with a head without hair and a face so destructively scabbed that the only possible identification method would be testing her DNA. She has a cloth casually tossed over her, not out of dignity for the dead but out of the sheer bother not to offend the living. I wonder who owns that.

Lala grips my hand, and I support her weight, which has begun to stoop and sway from nausea. We check all the bodies, row by row—the shriveled old ones that have been dead for years, the ones with tiny bullet-sized holes in their heads, the thoroughly roasted ones, and the ones sent to the great beyond through different, bizarre, slightly perceptible, and even inventive means—line by line, face by face. Vandra is not in any of them. Okay! So this means that the Lord is alive! Really alive!

We step out into the sunlight at last, refusing to tell the other that we feel better. Funny how these things happen. How I would condemn and instantly strike from the earth the man who caused that particular burnt girl's death but would give away without hesitance the lives of everyone in those rooms just to keep Vandra. How the world would suddenly have no meaning without my girl and how I, if I had the power, would enforce my will upon 7.7 billion others and wish for them to be dispensed with, just to let my little girl live. How heaven is somewhere I ceaselessly preach about yet find no solace in the probability that Vandra might have died and could likely be there now. The sun cleanses our lungs and melts the smell of formalin off our clothes and skin, and I hear Lala thanking the Lord for keeping his promises to us and keeping Vandra safe. I dial Vandra again when Lala is not looking. It almost seems as though the operator sighs a reply and goes back to sleep.

———

"The bodies were carried to three different mortuaries," the radio said, the telly said, the people said, and Facebook said. We make it to the third, the one owned by a hospital, the one that, if we don't see Vandra there, would seal our 'victory'. The passage into the mortuary has the kind of thin, brittle-y artificial hard-to-clean tiles from too cheap disinfectant soaked in too little water. The mortuary itself, though wide and clean, still has that unpleasant scent of formalin in the air, from which everything must be made. We walk into it, and we check, one body after the other, stifling dread and shock at the plastic eerie-sleepy stillness of what used to be people. Each body seen and passed is accompanied by a thought or a wonder, a small victory for Lala and I and more hope of life for Vandra. We scrutinize each face for signs of semblance. None. No Vandra. We walk through the mortuary hallway, trying not to smile (for it would be weird) or look relieved.

"I can feel it," Lala tells me. "She's alive. Vandra's alive." She doesn't know that. Her tone told me so, no clearer than a board lacking signs would have been.

Faith is a bastard. Hope is her tougher, crueler twin. Hope is the sky and the earth who both refuse you. Faith asks you to keep running through air until you see "a place between sky and earth" (which you are thinking is sky or earth). The more you run, the more you run. You cannot give up, not just because you have come so far but because you can still run, and things always turn up when you run. Luxury and necessity at once! That is what she is, she doesn't exist.

I have made a handful of friends here. It has been a strange thing, what is happening to us. Words are scarce because faces silently speak stories as clearly as voices. None of the stories are ever finished. We continue with our lips when our eyes finally fall shut. One of us, the one who still sees, his name is Pa Zuzu. Pa Zuzu lost his wife like I lost Lala: they woke up and just decided not to live again. No kids, the both of us. A plunge into and a pull from insanity is what our situations are sometimes. He still sees. I ask him to do something for me. It is something I have left for thirteen years. Something I stubbornly still turned my back on in this home, but now a poke from it makes me ask for it.

"Yes?"

There is something about Pa Zuzu's *s* that sounds clearer, more precise, and strangely tickling. I chuckle. He chuckles too out of courtesy.

"Would you help me dial something?"

I hear him shuffle around. He's looking for his cell, I suppose. I wait for him for a couple of seconds.

"Yes."

It is still imprinted in my memory. I have tried blotting it out, but even thirteen years of willful forgetfulness has done everything but make me forget. I call out the numbers slowly, without even thinking. Pa Zuzu says, "Okay?" I know he wants to dial when I confirm the big okay. Years have beaten down my strength and expectations into a dull pulse, so I listen in the silence between us with all the hope of a man who still undoubtedly expects to be disappointed. I somehow expect to hear that same operator. Or have they changed her? I can hear the connection crackling. The silence is unusually long, and each second stokes my curiosity and massages the dull pulse into a throb that …

It begins to ring.

My heartbeat ceases. In that second, I grasp at possibilities and an end, struggling through air, hoping to reach that place, hoping to get that closure. I fumble through and grab for the phone, huddling it to my ear. It rings. It keeps on ringing. Thirteen years! Thirteen years! It is her. I know it is.

A voice emerges after a slight, crinkly crackle. "Hello?"

The world around me gets caught in suspense. It is her. Years haven't taken anything from that voice.

"Vandra?" I stutter, reaching through air for the phone. My voice climbs. "Vandra! Can you hear me, Vandra? Vandra, it is Daddy, your father... hello … Vandra …"

There's long and contemplative silence. Then there's a slight ruffle, a short pause, and three beeps.

Acknowledgement

For the countless times I grew frustrated with my manuscript and doubted the authenticity of my gift, the times my infamous temper and juvenile impatience had the better of me and had me cursing the processes that led to the birth of this book, there was always Indira to tell me it was all very normal, and that she believed in my ability to pull it off. This book would never have been possible without her words, superhuman understanding, unconditional love and actions, most of which I've never sufficiently reciprocated or thanked her for. Mami, muchas gracias por todo. I hope I make you proud with this.

Nyore 'Bad Uncle' Gustavo has been my friend over thirteen years now, is the most selfless human I've ever met and I dare say, the most prolific raconteur I've listened to. Conversations between us spun numerous ideas, some of which found their way into this book, some of which have already found their way into the next book and of course, a lot of which will find their way into many more after that. Thanks a billion, brother. But do not let your head get too big for this does not make you any less of the idiot I see you as.

My mother, Helen Ovoke, has been the most influential figure in my life right from birth. There could be no me if there is no her. Mumsi, I say migwo. And my popsy, Benson Ejiro, for giving me a good education, I say migwo too.

To the staff, especially the editors at Archway Publishing, I say a big thank you too. And to my city, Warri, and the beauty in and of her people, last no be wetin we dey carry.

I say tuale!

About the Author

KI Jagoban is influenced, and heavily, by Richard Wright. Most of his stories lend his narrative style. I live everywhere and sometimes write all the time.